The Flag

By
Robbie Cottrell

3

By the same author

Mister Doggett
The Tidewaiter
The Arsonist
The Clergyman

Non-fiction

Thomas Doggett Coat & Badge
(300 plus years of history)
Much enlarged, covering 1715-2018

Suggested reading

The Coat
By Robert G.Crouch

THE FLAG

BY
ROBBIE COTTRELL

This book is based on fact, with a sprinkling of fiction. Roger De Flor and Ramon Muntaner did exist during a period of history where death was never too far away.

Rob & Carol Cottrell started their genealogy business in 1996.
Since then, they have
indexed in excess of one hundred Thames & Medway
riverside parishes, along with every apprenticeship binding
record of 1688 to 1959 for
Thames Watermen & Lightermen

This is Robert's sixth book, weaving the fabric of fact
within the beautiful framework of fiction.
Not bad for someone suffering with Parkinson's

He endeavours to prove there is life after Parkinson's.

PARKINSON'S UK
CHANGE ATTITUDES.
FIND A CURE.
JOIN US.

With gratitude to Dr Michael Samuel

'The Captain,'
by William Moody.

    This ship was originally named the *"Resolution"* before changing its name to the *"Rising Sun"*. It was primarily active in the Caribbean with 36 guns and 150 men aboard. Typically, they burned, stranded, and looted the ships they captured.

    But our story and the origins of the flag go back much further in time, back to 1305.

With special thanks to

Toni Mount, Ian Nicholson and the members
of the Gravesend Creative Writing Group

Toni Mount
My Mentor

Ian Nicholson
My overworked editor

Finally, my sincere thanks to Raymond Hudson,
an historian specialising in ancient Freemasonry.
I sincerely thank him for the Prologue to this book and
his suggestion of checking out the Chinon Document.

Background information

This book is based on fiction, with a sprinkling of fact mixed in for good measure. It is a fact the Roger De Flor and Ramon Muntaner existed during a period of history where blood was never far away.

It has never been my intention to instil fear and foreboding to the reader. However, in 1307 the Templars, the most ferocious fighting force the world had ever known was practically eliminated by the King of France and a French Pope.

It is a known fact that hundreds, if not thousands of Knights Templar were burnt at the stake In Paris, but many escaped, along with a fortune in gold. To this day the whereabouts of the gold remains unsolved.

What followed was a blood bath covering the whole of Europe - you know it today as The Hundred Year War.

The Hundred Years' War was fought between France and England during the late middle Ages. It lasted 116 years between 1337 and 1453. The war started because Charles IV of France died in 1328 without an immediate male heir (i.e., a son or younger brother). Edward III of England, then believed he had the right to become the new king of France through his mother.

The French did not want a foreign king, so Philip VI of France said he ought to be king because by the Salic law women could not rule or transmit the right to rule to their sons. The two countries went to war because of this disagreement.

Prologue

In the year 1099

'In the year 1099, nine Knights from Gaul, led by Godfrey de Bouillon entered Jerusalem, and befriended King Baldwin I to convince him to allow them to reside in the Temple grounds. There is archaeological proof that these knights tunnelled underneath the centre of the temple and possibly up into the level just below the Sanctum Sanctorum. They must have discovered something, and there are many legends speculating on what actually was found, because subsequently Hugh de Payens petitioned Baldwin II for permission for these nine knights to establish themselves as a new religious order. This permission was granted. They took the name "The Poor Fellow Soldiers of Christ and the Temple of Jerusalem. They became known by many titles, but were popularly remembered as Knights Templar. For the next nine years very little was recorded of their actions.

Neither did they take in any new recruits, rather strange for a new order. All these nine knights came from Champagne in Gaul, and most were closely related in some way. Through Bernard of Clairvaux, nephew to one of the nine and Abbott of the Cistercian Order, and later to be canonised as St Bernard, they obtained a Rule from the Pope. With the powerful religious backing of the Pope and the Holy Roman Catholic Church, Bernard of Clairvaux, known as the "Second Pope", and King Baldwin II of Jerusalem, they were now officially formed and recognised as such. They were not originally set up as an Order of Chivalry, but primarily as an escort of protection of the pilgrims making their way to the Holy Land. Whereas the Hospitallers or Knights of St John were formed to administer aid and succour to those pilgrims who fell foul to the many bandits on their route.'

Bernard championed their cause vociferously and urged that they be supported with gifts of land and money and encouraged aristocratic young men to forget their sinful lives and take up the sword and the cross as Templar Knights. So successful was his canvassing that the King of France gave both monies and substantial grants of land, which was promptly followed by similar gestures from the nobility. King Stephen of England did likewise. The knights were granted many productive manors which provided a continuous income.

So, Hugh de Payens had left Jerusalem as one of a small group of an obscure unofficial order, returning just two years later with 300 knights, the backing of the Pope and many of the kings of Europe, and untold wealth and land.

Over the next 200 years they were to become the most powerful and respected force in the then known world. They built preceptories and castles all over Europe and the Middle East. They were great builders responsible for tremendous cathedrals and churches, many of which still stand today. They also built up a tremendous fleet of ships, and conducted trade with spices and silks etc. Their fighting prowess was justifiably legendary. They were also skilled in commerce, law and financial matters, holding the treasuries of both England and France. Many European kings were in their financial debt, especially King Phillip of France. They were considered experts in law and helped to structure the legal system of England at the time. Their main preceptor, and the surrounding area, in London, is still steeped in the legal profession..

At their zenith of power and wealth, as is always the case, envy became the bed for malicious rumour. Their secret rites, initiations and ceremonies were speculated to be blasphemous. Phillip, King of France saw this as an opportunity to grab their wealth and power, and therefore automatically absolve himself of his huge

15

financial debt to them, he conspired with the Pope, whom history proves was in actual fact his puppet, to decimate the Order on charges of heresy. To all of which the Pope agreed. This was effected in absolute secrecy, so that on Friday the 13th October 1307, 5,000 Knights Templar were arrested and imprisoned in France. This date (Friday the 13th) has held fear and dread for many people ever since, although the origins have become lost in the mist of time. When the arresting soldiers went to take charge of their fleet of ships in La Rochelle, it had gone, together with the Templar treasury, so the secrecy could not have been as absolute as was believed.

Recopied by kind permission of R.W.Hudson

Chapter One

1304/5

La Rochelle
France

The cloudless night sky over La Rochelle, where the Templar fleet lay at anchor within the deep harbour, looked both spellbinding and captivating. The days had been relatively calm with very little wind and no rain for good measure. 'Let's be glad of small mercies,' thought Roger de Flor, the part Sicilian part German fleet captain, as he carefully negotiated the gangplank that connected his vessel to the Quayside. Ramon Muntaner, his Catalan second in command, followed close behind and George Ward, a brute of an Englishman of inferior birth, brought up the trio. George knew that De Flor had been raised through the ranks from cabin boy to sergeant through to the extreme heights of a captain within the Templar fleet. News had recently come to La Rochelle regarding the probable crack down on Templar activities, even to the extent of false charges being brought forward by the King and the Church whereby the Knights Templar fraternity might be disqualified from the rules and laws of the Crown and Church. If these unfounded charges blossomed upon fertile ground, it would spell the demise and erasure of the Templars from the face of the earth. However, not all secrets remain secret; there is normally always a weak link somewhere in the chain of command, and a loose word here suddenly re-appears on the lips of someone not to be trusted often causes trouble and the rupture of the secret becomes shattered. Such appears to be the King's orders to arrest and confine the Templars to the Kings dungeons.

The best-laid plans of mice and men often go awry!

The trio made their way to the old quarter of La Rochelle where the waterfront taverns were rowdy and raucous. De Flor pushed through the doors of 'The Mermaid' his favourite ale and wine tavern. As he did there was a marked silence, as if the three men were Muslims walking into a Crusader encampment, which of course could not have been further from the truth. They may not have been from the military wing of the Crusader army, but they were equal in prowess and all three deserved a far better welcome. Perhaps the news from the King of France had already found ears willing to listen within the Mermaid.

The landlord strolled over to where the three men sat to take their order. Muntaner was puzzled by the lack of respect shown to them from their fellow drinkers. The landlord appeared ill at ease when he took their order of three large glasses of his finest wine accompanied by a generous portion of French ham. De Flor couldn't help but notice the landlord's right hand shaking with unease and carefully placed his right hand atop that of the landlord to indicate he needed to talk. De Flor had a jovial way of extracting information from those who found free speech hard to complete. De Flor was in need of additional information, and within no time at all, the landlord whispered that it would be best if the trio drank elsewhere for their own safety.

'My dear friend Ramon', Roger edged closer to his friend, 'you have Catalan blood, and you have skirmished with your French landlord longer than necessary just tell him you will take your custom elsewhere, before punching him on the mouth. I am from Brindisi, which as you know is within the Kingdom of Sicily. George is our friend, although he hasn't a clue what blood runs through his veins, I wouldn't be surprised if he knows its colour, let alone know his father. Let us eat and drink awhile whilst we judge the character of the landlord's fellow guests, we wouldn't want to cause a disturbance within this cosy establishment.'

Ramon suggested that an additional chair should be brought to the table to allow the landlord to update them on recent activities within the Atlantic French port of La Rochelle, and what, if any, is the latest news from Paris. George rested his huge hand on the landlord's left hand to persuade him to linger awhile.

The landlord looked alarmed and shaken, he tried to break free from George's grip, but the match was completely one sided leaving the landlord little choice but to sit with his newly arrived customers and chew the cud; whilst drinkers sitting nearby tried their best to make sure they didn't miss a single syllable that was spoken between the landlord and his guests.

George requested to know the landlord's name. 'It is disrespectful not to be aware of whom we speak.'

The landlord quaking in fear answered, 'My name is Philip. I am named after our King,' he quickly replied. 'You know us well, Philip,' George continued

George looked deep into the landlord's weary eyes as he tried to continue with his conversation 'As a good friend, I must tell you that I detect sinister motives afoot, within your establishment.'

The landlord looked on the verge of fouling his pants. 'It's just that,' he said in trying to resume the conversation, 'It's just that,' he repeated.

'It's just what?' George asked. Ramon and Roger were silently enjoying what was being played out in front of them, taking great pleasure in the fact that the landlord had started to dig a big a much bigger hole for himself, and no matter how hard he tried to manoeuvre the conversation away from George, the hole got bigger.

The landlord whispered to Ramon. 'I am going to the kitchen. Please follow me in a couple minutes.'

Philip left the table and leisurely walked into the tavern's kitchen. Ramon followed soon after, but after a few seconds he reappeared wearing a look of astonishment and anger. 'Let's go, gentlemen.'

Roger and George were tucking into their excellent ham and finishing their wine when Ramon spoke with urgency.

'That ain't a suggestion. I really think we need to move quickly in case one of these scumbags wants his ale topped up,' Roger enquired, 'what's the problem,' to which Ramon answered that the fucking landlord's dead.

Roger joked about the landlord's sudden death. 'I see you haven't lost your touch, but did you winkle anything out of the fool?' Ramon looked shocked at Roger's suggestion. 'I didn't cut his throat! It appears that someone doesn't want us to hear what Philip wanted to impart.'

George enquired if the man had been murdered or if there had been an accident. 'I don't think too many Quayside landlords with a profitable business would be in the habit of cutting their own throat. They make too much money selling their watered-down ale and wine, not to mention the rotten stale food at exorbitant prices.

No, someone wanted to make sure Philip kept quiet.'

George offered a suggestion. 'Let's quickly return to 'The Falcon' and check if any of the crew has noticed recent disharmony within the port.'

Ramon Muntaner spent most of the night speaking with the crew, or those crewmembers that are still aboard, and was surprised to hear the intelligence obtained. 'I think you and I have to be more careful and shouldn't go ashore unaccompanied, especially at night in La Rochelle. It seems there is a price on his head.

What the men have learned is that the death warrants for Jacque de Molay and Roger de Flor were signed from someone on high.'

'How high?' George asked.

'Damn highest in the land,' Ramon replied.

'Such as?' George remained steadfast. He wanted an answer to his question and just like a dog with a bone he wouldn't let go.

'What do you get when you mix the Pope with the King?' Ramon countered.

'A right Royal fuck up,' George quickly laughed. 'It seems we have gained too many enemies by growing richer than the Church or King. The Pope and the King of France owe us more than they can repay. Hence the easiest way to get out of your dilemma is to eliminate the banker, and make yourself debt free.'

Roger recalled that oft-untold tale about the Richard Plantagenet slaughtering nearly three thousand hostages at Acre simply because he was impatient and didn't trust Saladin; 'that's another way of bypassing your dilemma's,' he said.'

Ramon looked perplexed, but Roger had an answer. 'At least when you fight a Muslim you know who you are fighting. There are too many bloody backstabbers around today.'

George looked at both his friends and clapped his hands together to get their attention. 'I fear that there will never be peace in the Holy Land when we have despots as leaders, and I can foresee war until the end of time within God's Kingdom. None of us will die in cosy feather beds, and I fear we all will die in the blood-soaked sands of Jerusalem.'

After the fall of Acre, Richard Plantagenet wanted to exchange a large number of Muslim prisoners being held at Ayyadieh for the True Cross. Rumour has it that a deal was struck between Richard and Saladin, with a deadline set for the Islamic warlord to fulfil his side of the bargain which included a gift of 100,000 gold pieces in the exchange of 1,600 Christians held captive by Saladin.

The Muslim chronicler Baha ad-Din, writing from inside Saladin's camp, indicated that many of the crusaders disapproved of Richard's actions, and couldn't understand why Richard ordered the executions.

Sections of the Muslim Army became so enraged by the killings that they attempted to charge the Crusader lines, but were repeatedly beaten back, allowing Richard's forces to retire in good order.

Richard Plantagenet oversaw the execution of nearly three thousand Muslim captives at Ayyadieh.

Chapter Two

1305
Adrianople

Roger had always held doubts appertaining to the Holy Land and its incessant wars. First, he had not considered them particularly 'Holy', and secondly, in his view, the wars were only making the king and barons immensely rich. The common foot soldiers, if they survived the battle, had to rely on looting of the dead to obtain their wages.

Besides being the leader of the Great Catalan Company, Roger was a great strategist, and after studying his maps of the eastern Mediterranean, Roger instinctively knew that whoever held this relatively moderate-sized portion of water would hold one of the largest trading routes in the palm of his hands. From every point of the ship's compass Roger sensed rich pickings, and if he realised it, other European powers would see it, and Islam would eagerly recognise the golden opportunities it held, as would the far eastern countries of Asia. There had already been too many

European powers ready to fight over supremacy of trade routes and some had much louder voices than others.

Ramon viewed the maps once more before silently agreeing with Roger. All he had to say was just four simple words - 'survival of the fittest'. With that brief but true statement, the three friends sailed once more for the turbulent waters of Cyprus.

George always had a simple view of what was going on around him, and often explained to De Flor that he could never understood why, over the decades, the silent majority had not realised that compromise didn't mean victory or defeat for either side. Since the initial crusade too many good men, from both sides of the great faith divide, had gone to whatever God they prayed to in misery and agony, their corpses improperly defiled and robbed by looters. What in the name of heaven had the Crusaders been fighting for? He understood the priests pushed them forward promising them a place in ecstasy above due to their fighting in the name of God; Urging them to kill as many Muslims as possible to win a place in heaven. If they were all fighting for God, he must be very confused whose side he was on.

De Flor and Mutainer always considered the worthless strip of sand known as God's Kingdom to be both poor and infertile; nothing much grew on its bleak landscape. At one time Muslims, Jews and Christians lived together in harmony, but now that rocky, sandy vastness of the Judean desert was good for nothing but fighting and dying.

The principle deception of the Holy Land was to secure a comfortable seat as near to God's side in whatever interpretation they had in heaven or paradise, depending on what book your faith guides. Roger de Flor trusted no-one; to him the congregations were gullible fools.

At eight years of age Roger de Flor went to sea in a galley belonging to the Knights Templar. He entered the order and eventually became captain of a galley called 'El Falcó'.

Following the rescue of wealthy survivors from the siege of Acre by the Mamluk Sultan Al-Ashraf Khalil ten years ago, De Flor based himself in Cyprus. However, following some intrigues and personal disputes with the locals he was accused of robbery and denounced to the Pope as a thief and an apostate. This type of treachery failed to stop De Flor's antics, but it did make for enemies. Whilst in Cyprus, Roger employed food and drink tasters, which proved highly fortunate for De Flor. His chroniclers, over the years, recorded in excess of thirty tasters meeting a premature death by reason of poisoned food or drink meant for Roger's plate or goblet.

On his return from Cyprus, De Flor attended a grand reception at Adrianople, to the west of Constantinople in Turkey, under an alias. Due to his deep suspicions of not trusting the Turks; Roger had taken the precaution of being accompanied by a body-double.

Once the fatal melee got underway the assassin slashed out blindly, cutting the wrong man's throat. Sensing danger, De Flor had already vacated the scene with two of his trusted bodyguards, leaving the body-double cold and lifeless, but this ill-fated treacherous left hundreds dead in the aftermath of the assassination attempt. Thereafter the Company avenged itself, plundering from Macedonia to Thrace in what became known as the 'Catalan Vengeance'. Death and vengeance for De Flor was simple, because by preserving the lie of his murder the former Sicilian commander of the Catalan brigade, it left Roger free and unopposed to take charge of guarding the Grand Master and intercepting every message coming out of the Royal Palace.

Even as early as 1305 rumours were spreading concerning the newly elected French Pope and the King of France. Both Ramon and Roger knew it and George would in time witness it for himself. If the rumours came to fruition, it would mean the end of the Templar system in general and its Grand Master, Jacque de Molay, the man who managed the order of warrior monks for the past seven years.

De Molay ruled over the dying days of the Knights Templar system. Support from European nations dwindled to such an extent that the order was essentially confined to France.

Roger and Ramon obtained reliable intelligence from a Royal source who spoke too freely, especially whilst under the influence of French alcohol. From as early as 1306 the French Pope Clement V and King Philip IV, were about to negotiate yet another financial loan with the Templar bankers, which they had no intention of repaying, although the loan would solve France's immediate bankruptcy problems. It seems dishonourable to think the loan should be borrowed from the identical source they intended to annihilate. Meanwhile, gossip was spreading fast regarding the impending arrest of De Molay and every French Templar.

Most of Europe knew only too well that the reason for the imminent arrest of Jacque de Molay was judged on pure greed and jealously. A Papal bull had been announced that all of Europe should comply with Rome's declaration, but few bothered, some openly denied the authority of the Catholic Church and the debt-ridden French King leaves them both isolated in the knowledge of their murderous intentions. Thus, after many deliberations The Crown and the Church theorised the quickest and easiest way to rid themselves of their financial predicament was to forcibly close the Templars Bank, remove the bank's assets, and eliminate the previously untouchable Templars from the face of earth and water. The plan seemed foolproof, except the schemers forgot about the will and reaction of the people. The Templars had freely given alms to the sick and needy, so when faced with the probability of alms drying up due to a gluttonous King, open revolt might follow.

The Templars may have lost their purpose as a war machine, but they still controlled vast wealth and, as a consequence of that huge wealth, Pope Clement V proposed to fabricate charges against both the Templars and Jacque de Molay. These charges included heresy, homosexuality, financial corruption, fraud, devil worshipping, spitting on the cross and much more.

Roger de Flor received secret intelligence, whether it is true or not, that King Philip fought to oppose these charges, but the newly elected French Pope had only one thing on his mind, the death of Jacque de Molay and the destruction of the Knights Templar order. The Templars banking system had grown immensely stronger and richer than the crown and the church. Roger and Ramon tried in vain to warn Molay of the sheer gravity of his situation, but on Friday the thirteen day of October 1307 rumour turned to reality and hundreds of French Templars were arrested and imprisoned.

Over the decades the Templars had gained a pious reputation as the poor soldiers of Christ. Pope Innocent II issued a Papal Bull that allowed the Knights Templar special rights. Among them, the Templars were exempt from paying taxes, permitted to build their own oratories, and obey no-one except the Pope.

George appeared perplexed when he asked De Flor if the King considered any of the charges leveled at the Grand Master to be true, as they all seemed far-fetched.

Everyone knew the French King was financially indebted to the Templars and although their money was ordered to be passed over to the Knights Hospitallers, stories abounded to tell there was no love lost between the two wings, so with that out in the open it is safe to say no transfer of funds ever took place between the two, although Philip and King Edward II of England retained a sizeable sum for themselves.

Philip was severely irritated, but his greatest frustration was the disappearance of a great horde of wealth removed from the Paris Temple Bank. It was said to be loaded on a wagon train departing from the

Atlantic port of La Rochelle where the Templars fleet was moored or anchored within the bay.

Roger surmised the capture of the Templars must be carried out with supreme haste and many had already befallen in captivity, torture or death.

De Flor slammed his gloved fist on the table to point out the obvious. 'We don't have time on our side! These wagons are still struggling across France under our faithful escort.' No one knows what secrets those wagons hold except for De Molay, Ramon and me.

Not a living soul, save for the Templars Bank and a few loyal trusted men of whom we are three, we're aware of the existence of the convoy and its cargo. Ramon set out some facts to the others. 'We have eighteen ships, fifty horses, and over six hundred men waiting to sail to clandestine destinations chosen specifically by De Molay.'

It was George's turn to point out the obvious. 'Until the wagon train arrives from Paris we have nowhere to go. We must be patient and hope our prayers are answered. The wagons should arrive before sunrise tomorrow, otherwise all our skullduggery will have been in vain.'

'George, you take first watch and wake us when the gold arrives.'

At four o'clock George reported the arrival of the first wagon. The sun had yet to show its face to the world when the convoy of loaded wagons abruptly halted in line alongside La Rochelle's Quayside. Everyone remained anxious until all the cargo was safely secured and lashed down beneath the wooden hatch boards of the various vessels. Roger gave sealed written orders to each of his eighteen captains before setting sail, and to assist security De Molay gave orders to divide the fleet into four separate smaller squadrons. De Molay's thinking being if one group was captured the other three would be unable to inform their interrogators where the others were headed.

At six-thirty every ship was ready to set sail. Roger needed to put as many miles between the French port and his eighteen ships as humanly possible. Ramon and George hoped to put at least one hundred miles between La Rochelle and the Templar fleet, but Roger wanted more.

Not everyone aboard the little flotilla was under De Flor's direct command; over fifty Templars were saved from a brutal death, as well as a few Germans, three Englishmen, twelve Italians, twenty-three Spaniards, three Jews and four Portuguese. Curiously Roger had neglected to tell his captains that fifty Muslim loyal to De Flor had been spread about his ships which he intensively didn't mention for safety reasons, until they were well on their way.

One thing was for sure. Ramon was at his happiest when sailing with Roger and George. Once outside the harbour Roger told his friends that he had enlisted the fifty Arabs.

'We are all nations less and outlawed from society. As far as I am concerned, it is far better to be outlawed than to live in permanent fear of receiving a knock on the door, which could mean the Pope's secret guard or the King's men taking you and your family prisoner and locking them up within their private prisons and torturing them for information.'

France had never been pushed so close to the edge through self-preservation before. Roger thought about those four words Ramon had spoken earlier - 'survival of the fittest.' Perhaps in the years ahead of me, he mused, someone far greater than me will make use of that phrase

Roger, George and Ramon stood on the poop deck of 'The Falcon', each with a goblet in their hand ready to offer a toast.

'To our Grand Master, whom we sincerely trust will live longer than this night.'

'Best cast off, gentlemen, but before we set sail let us salute the flag you now fly under.' Roger gave a haughty laugh, but Ramon and George were unable to see the flag or why De Flor was being secretive. The night sky remained black and unrevealing, and the sun had yet to make its appearance on the western horizon. The night clouds hadn't shifted and kept Roger's symbolic flag invisible a little longer.

Ramon's view of this flag remained concealed, although he thought, knowing De Flor as he did, the flag had to be emblematic of Roger's inner self and beliefs. Suddenly, Ramon and George stood transfixed, screwing their eyes on a position high up on the main mast. Both men were unexpectedly startled when somewhere ashore the cocks crowed in unison, beginning their disruptive dawn chorus. Right on cue, the clouds slowly drifted inshore to offer a brief glimpse of Roger's mysterious flag.

Ramon was shocked. 'In God's name, I've never seen anything like that in my lifetime! What the hell is the symbolism behind this flag? It looks more like the devil than a flag of God. I cannot see any association with Christ with that abomination, and the people will not understand your motives. Surely it would be better to sail under the cross.'

Ramon continued to glare at De Flor's face, hoping for a reaction.

'All in good time my friends, all in good time, but I'll tell you this - it is highly symbolic. One day soon all will be explained, but I assure you all it is the most suitable and beautiful explanation of Christ.'

Ramon and George were impatient, but they knew better than to push Roger any further on the point. If he promised everything in good time, then when the time was right, he would indeed explain it all to them.

With their goblets empty, the three men returned to their cramped quarters aboard 'The Falcon'. George and Ramon remained shocked, while Roger laughed in merriment.

George enquired about the Templars and the Hospitallers, he knew the Templars were covered with a religious veneer applied covering the 'warrior-monks' and they're often remarkably courageous and sometimes excessively brutal feats which were perceived and advertised as 'acts of love'. George knew about their fighting and maritime arms, but not that much about its banking, rural husbandry and building arms, those behind the building arm were known as 'The Children of Solomon'.

As for the Knights Hospitallers, their extended military arm helped to bolster the autonomous political and economic domains not only in the Outremer but also the Levant and across Europe.

To the left King Philip IV of France,
To the right Pope Clement V

Chapter Three

1306
Malta

Messages were flying in and out La Rochelle by homing pigeons, informing De Flor of his enemies' progress. It was shortly after eight o'clock when a message arrived, explaining that the King was less than twenty miles from the port. De Flor's small fleet was only ten miles offshore when he gathered his captains together for one last briefing on orders; although De Molay left strict instructions they should be kept secret regarding their separate destinations. Molay had confided in Roger so he knew the exact locations as to where the ships should wait.

De Molay wanted at least six ships to sail on a westerly course to a land that the Muslims and Spanish Moors within his crew called America. It was usually referred to as the New World, although some identified the land as Amerigo Vespucci after the Italian explorer, financier, navigator, and cartographer. Vespucci was born in the Republic of Florence.

De Flor listened intently as the Muslims and Italians in his party spoke of vast forests, lush valleys, lakes and meandering rivers. They said that the majority of the land mass appeared uninhabited, save for a few savages. De Flor suggested that it would be straight forward to establish settlements in this new land where a man could be self-sufficient. The sailors all agreed that once the community had been established, some could return to Europe, bringing with them their wives and children.

De Flor considered this an excellent course of action. All they had to do to keep sailors under control was to help them with the supply of land, drink, food and most importantly women.

Roger continued passing orders to the captains of the second group. Ever mindful of the King's pursuit, he kept one eye to the east, where the sun was rising. Five ships would sail south, passing the southern tip of Africa is known as Kaap de Goede Hoop, or as George his sailing master translated, 'The Cape of God Hope.' Once the Cape was rounded they would enter the calmer waters of the Indian Ocean, then sail on a northerly tack to a vast island that lay off the African coast known as Madagascar. Ramon Muntaner viewed Madagascar with caution, as he associated the inhabitants and their traditions with the slave islands in the Caribbean. Ramon was profoundly concerned when he told his fellow captains that he had heard that the native population were mainly lawless individuals brought to the Thousand Island Crescent, known collectively as the Caribbean. Their roots were mainly African, and before they arrived on the great island nothing in terms of culture or true faith existed.

De Flor explained that the small fleet should sail further north where the terrain and climate were more suited to European tastes.

With eleven vessels now accounted for, De Flor turned to Ramon Muntaner, and spoke in a quiet voice so as not to be overheard. 'In you my friend I put my greatest faith and trust. I wish you to sail with six of our ships to the north of England, to a savage worthless place like Scotland. The exact location where I wish you to anchor is just off the high granite town known as Dùn Èideann. That name is in Scottish Gaelic, but our English brethren know the place as the Burgh of Eidyn or as the Scottish King now calls it Edinburgh.'

Ramon looked shocked. 'What about you?'

'I will sail with George in the Mediterranean, where I hold lands. After all am I not the Count of Malta.'

Ramon remained opened mouth as he spluttered out his objection. 'Roger, you will be sailing right into the arms of the King and the Pope! Why the hell do you wish to sail to Malta? The King will have his spies tracking every vessel that sails inwards through the straights of Mount Tariq.'

'Shit to the King, I say! He has dishonoured the name of France. I have to sail to Malta to collect some personal effects important to me.'

'At least let me go with you,' Ramon insisted.

'My dear friend,' De Flor tearfully replied, 'You have no idea how important your mission is. Please wait for me at Eidyn at the mouth of the Leith River. I will join you within thirty-six months, but if I fail to return don't come looking for me.'

Ramon Muntaner wanted to continue his argument with his friend, but knew once De Flor had made up his mind, nothing could change it. 'I don't see the importance of Malta, Roger, but if your mind is made up so be it.' 'What I hope to return to having great importance, more significant than the Holy Grail itself.'

The first mention of the grail appears in the incomplete poem *The Story of the Grail,* written between 1180 and 1191, but said grail has no holiness or mythological properties. It wasn't until the grail appeared again in Robert de Boron's verse romance *Joseph d'Arimathie* between 1191 and 1202 that the grail or 'chalice' is linked to Christ, claiming that the sacred cup was used in the last supper and to collect Christ's blood on the cross.

Artist's impression of the Holy Grail, or chalice.

Chapter Four

1307-1314
Friday the 13th October 1307

Secret documents had been sent by couriers throughout France. The papers included lurid details and whispers of black magic and scandalous sexual rituals. They were sent by King Philip IV of France, an avaricious monarch who in the preceding years had launched an attack on a powerful banking group named Lombard's. He had also expelled France's Jews, so he could confiscate their property for his depleted coffers.

In the days and weeks that followed that fateful Friday, more than fifteen thousand Templars were arrested, including the Grand Master Jacques de Molay, and the Order's treasurer. While some of the highest-ranking members were caught up in Philip's net, however, so too were hundreds of non-warriors. These were middle-aged men who managed the day-to-day banking and farming activities that kept the organization humming and were faced with many charges.

The Templars were kept in isolation and fed meagre rations that often amounted to just bread and water. Nearly all were brutally tortured. One common practice used by medieval inquisitors was the 'strappdo,' in which the hands of the accused were tied behind their backs, and then suspended in the air by a rope around their wrists, intended to dislocate the shoulders.

The hands of one imprisoned Templar were tied so tightly that blood pooled in his fingertips, he was kept in a pit no wider than a single footstep. Many of the men were likely to be stretched on the infamous rack, or had their feet dipped in oil and held over a fire to burn. Given the extreme conditions, it's not surprising that within weeks, hundreds of Templars confessed to false charges, including Jacques de Molay.

Roger De Flor received messages aboard his ship, 'The Falcon', on a near weekly basis, keeping him up to date on the barbarism dealt out to his fellow Templars. Roger and his sailing Master George Ward swore an oath to eliminate as many of their friends' torturers as humanly possible. In addition, if either the King or the Pope came within the range of their crossbows, they would have no hesitation in firing theirs bolts.

Roger had nothing but loathing for France. Up until a few months ago, he called it safe and homely.

Then he would willingly have given up his life for the Templars and France, but nowadays that love had turned sour. France, he felt, was rotten to the core.

Pope Clement V had second thoughts on the barbarism inflicted on the Templars and was horrified that much of Philip's hatred and greed would tarnish his papacy. Although he'd been elected almost solely because of Philip's influence, he feared crossing the extremely popular Templars. The Knight's coerced 'confessions', however, forced his hand. Philip, who had anticipated Clement's reaction, made sure the false allegations against the Templars included detailed descriptions of their supposed heresy, counting on the gossiper, salacious accounts to carry weight within the Church. Clement issued a Papal bull ordering the Kings of Europe to arrest Templars living on their land. Roger was pleased that only a few answered their Papal request, but the fate of the French Templars had already been sealed. Their lands and money were confiscated and officially dispersed to another religious order, the Hospitallers, although greedy Philip did get his blood-soaked hands on some of the cash he'd coveted.

Within weeks of their confessions, many of Templars recanted, and Clement shut down the inquisition trials until 1308. The Templars lingered in their cells for two years before Philip had more than fifty of them burned at the stake in 1310. Two years later,

Clement formally dissolved the Order, although he did carry out the so-called Royal Order without passing judgment on the guilt. All it took was a signature on an execution warrant to seal their fate, and they'd be guilty as charged.

In the wake of King Philip's termination of the Templars, some men again confessed in the hope of gaining their freedom, while others died in captivity. France was soaked in innocent blood on the orders of the so-called Philip the Fair, a name far removed from the actual man.

Convinced that as King he ruled as God's divinely anointed representative, he locked himself in a fierce power struggle with the papacy. In 1305, he coaxed the election of Clement V, whom he hoped to manipulate.

In 1309, Clement V transferred his residence to Avignon, beginning what became known as the Babylonian Captivity of the Popes. In 1281 Philip increased his powers by marrying Joan of Navarre. The marriage wasn't overly happy, and Queen Joan died in 1305, allegedly from childbirth, whilst others were not overly convinced. The Bishop Guichard of Troyes, however, was arrested in 1308 and accused of killing the Queen with the help of witchcraft by sticking an image of her with a pin.

King Philip IV of France had formed when it came to trumped-up charges against those who crossed his path. Pope Boniface VIII refused to be bullied by the French king, so Philip unleashed his secretive and formidable slanderous machines to characterize the pontiff as a heretic, sodomite, wizard and magician. This was clearly an example of the king's bullying of a French bishop, which suggests the crimes against the Templars were false. A king who wanted somebody to disappear from society would have gotten his own way by means of his advisers spreading rumours to set about total character assassination. These constant accusations would continue until the Bishop or Pope was forced out of office or submitted to the King's will.

The die had been cast regarding the French Templars. Meanwhile, King Robert the Bruce of Scotland was supportive of the Templars offering protection to any that lived under Scottish law in exchange for a military alliance.

Ramon Muntaner, your Chronicler, claimed the credit behind the Scottish army's victory at Bannockburn did not solely rest with the Scots, but with a band of Templar knights from overseas. As most of them were fully aware that they were going to be arrested, they escaped over the French border. Roger considered the Templars flight and surmised there were only two countries they really could escape to, Portugal and

Scotland. In the case of Scotland no Papal bull was ever sent there, as the whole country had previously been excommunicated and consequently the directive would have proved non-effectual.

Jacque De Molay was a formidable strategist, and Roger De Flor knew the workings of Molay's skills more than anyone. He explained his plan of sending his fleet to Scotland, where the Templars would be welcomed as loyal and crucial allies.

Meanwhile, two significant facts were slowly taking place. Jacque de Molay was incarcerated in a stinking French prison, when during the middle of March 1314, a royal commission of three cardinals condemned Molay and other leading dignitaries of the order to a perpetual imprisonment. On hearing this sentence, Molay again retracted his confession; much to the fury of the Crown King Philip finally punished the imprisoned Templars with burning. On the precise orders of the King; Molay, as relapsed heretic was ordered to be burnt at the stake by King Philip IV's officers. Subsequently Molay was burnt at the stake on the nineteenth day of March 1314 alongside other prominent Templars, one being the Treasurer of the Order.

Secondly, Roger de Flor had sighted his homeland of Malta which lay just south of the island of Sicily. It seemed near improbable that his ship has sailed south through the great pillars of Hercules, known today as Mount Tariq. Roger had expected French spies to monitor his easterly progress through the Mediterranean, but everything remained silent. King Philip must have known that the Templar fleet at La Rochelle had disappeared along with the entire supply of gold hurriedly transferred from the Templar Bank in Paris. He knew the Templar fleet of La Rochelle had recently sailed from The Atlantic port of La Rochelle and he knew he had to intercept the gold, but the King had one problem - he had no idea of the destination of the Templar fleet. Roger hoped that his one solitary ship might complete his task, whereas a reasonable convoy of maybe fifteen ships would attract suspicions.

La Rochelle harbour entrance

There had been a widespread belief that the knights had discovered and kept religious artefacts and relics, such as the Holy Grail, the Ark of the Covenant and parts of the cross of Christ's crucifixion. Numerous other ideas and myths existed about the Knights Templar secret operations. One theory considered by the Templars involved in a conspiracy to preserve the bloodline of Jesus Christ. There's no question that the Knights Templar provoked intrigue and fascination that will probably continue until the end of time.

Ramon, however, wondered what possession Roger had brought to Malta and had safely hidden, and now risked his life to bring it back to Scotland instead of leaving it where he had hidden it to be found by the followers of King Philip IV or Pope Clement. Whatever it was, Ramon knew the relic must hold supreme power, like the Ark of the Covenant, or perhaps the spear of Longinus, known as the spear of destiny, or even Christ's face impregnated on a sheet on linen. In addition, he also knew that he had to be patient and wait for the return of his dear friend Roger De Flor.

The spear was said to have been discovered by Helena the mother of Constantine the Great, who melted it down and had it made into a helmet for her son and a bridle for his horse. However, no evidence of this ever has been proved.

The Spear of Destiny, the Turin Shroud,
and the Ark of the Covenant.

All Roger had to do was locate this hidden relic, re-board his ship and sail westerly through the Mount of Tariq before sailing northwards, keeping the coastline of France out of sight before entering the channel. He would then sail on a mainly northerly course to Leith and a fond reunion with Ramon Muntaner.

Roger had taken two men ashore with him to act as lookouts as well as to cover his back. Roger's small estate stood on the north-west coast of the small Mediterranean island known as Malta. His small estate was built adjacent to the old temple of Bugibba which dated back to prehistoric times and today stands like a bundle of boulders brought crashing down to earth by natural catastrophes. As a young boy Roger loved to play within the ruins with his many friends, but that was until he was eight years old and found himself friendless aboard a Templar ship. Roger was very resourceful and climbed steadily up from the bilges to stand firmly on the afterdeck of the 'The Falcon' as Captain.

'The Falcon' had returned to Malta. She sat off Mellieha Bay with one single anchor lying atop the sandy sea bottom about fifteen feet below, in readiness for a speedy retreat.

Overlooking the area, Roger couldn't miss the Selmun Palace, built by the Knights of Malta, Who were the Knights Hospitalleroriginally, during the reign of Grand Master Manoel de Rohan. The Palace was built both as a hunting lodge and noble residence. It not only had acres of grounds attached to it, but also boasted spectacular views across Mellieha and beyond, not that Roger had come back to admire these. In the small bay, 'The Falcon' lay silently at anchor, in view of someone who chose to look in the right direction.

However, today the Palace and his childhood home lay in disrepair, uninhabited save for a few goats who gratefully settled within the ruins during the night hours.

De Flor found the grounds of his old home guarded by six men, no doubt under the pay of the Pope or King. It made sense to De Flor that the King or the Pope would choose Malta or Sicily as a likely place of sanctuary. Roger calmly asked his two companions to climb further up the rugged rock formations to enquire the nature of the men who strolled in full view about the grounds. De Flor held his spyglass to his right eye, hoping for a better view. He had no idea what his men were talking about, but one thing was certain these so-called guards failed to carry any weapon.

One of Roger's men hailed him to come up and join them. If this was a trap De Flor was ready with a pair of pistols, two swords and two daggers. His hands caressed the instruments of war as if he fondled a woman's body, and the thought brought a glimpse of a smile to his mouth. Deciding it was safe for him to continue his climb; he reached the summit in no time, although he was breathing heavily. Roger's companion introduced the six men as local goat herders who were simply grazing their heard within the shelter of the ruined buildings. Roger was extremely civil to his new friends and offered to pay for three of his goats. A bargain was struck at an inflated price, but Roger didn't want to create friction between the two groups. Before telling his new friends that he wished to stay a while to look around his old home, he brought up an important subject. He asked if any of them had seen any strangers poking around the island or the village of Bugibba in particular. The six men looked at each other and began whispering to themselves, and a mild argument ensued before the allotted spokesperson came forward. He told Roger that a small company of soldiers had come to the island six weeks ago and as far as he knew they had all gone south for the livelier town of Valetta.

Across the goat track from Mellieha is the small and tranquil grotto, which brought wonderful memories flooding into Roger's mind. He walked towards the cavern entrance, through a small opening and down a flight of steps. He hoped that every pilgrim who walked past was unaware of what lay beneath their feet. A place of pilgrimage, the rear walls were lined with handwritten letters of gratitude and prayers. This was a perfect place to sit in silence, light a candle and collect your thoughts, but Roger had to collect a hidden package that had lain inside the cave since the fall of Acre. The heavy package didn't look particularly important, but when Roger held it in his arms a tear rolled down his cheek. His mission was partially complete.

Roger held his breath and kept his eyes tightly shut as he tried to remove himself from the real world. He was in a state of feeling close to his maker, and in a way he was.

Returning to the sunlight Roger heard sounds of shouting and alarm, realising that soldiers must have seen 'The Falcon' and returned for a fight. De Flor and his loyal two crew members slithered down the rock face to the beach below to where their tender boat was partially hidden. They got to the tender in record time and rowed as if the Devil himself were chasing them. Once aboard 'The Falcon' they felt safe. The anchor was lifted and with a slight favourable wind the ship was manoeuvred around to face the open sea. Now we have a choice to make. Either to sail north around Gozo and back to Mount Tariq and the open ocean, or go south, passing Valetta, Zonqor, Birzebbuga and on to the northerly town of Cirkewwa, before retracing their voyage back to The Pillars of Hercules at Mount Tariq. Roger contemplated his choice before thinking he should sail northwards and onwards to the west.

George Ward, his sailing master, thought long and hard about his friend's decision before speaking up. 'It'll be a bloody hard sail for the next three or four days as I fear there'll be a heavy storm coming our way.'

Roger was unperturbed. 'If there's a storm for us, there will equally be a storm for our pursuers.'

Although he didn't say anything else, Roger wondered if he had made the right choice. However, it had been made now, so 'The Falcon' sailed north to

Gozo and beyond. As his brain was churning for the correct answer, he held on tightly to the old scruffy brick-built contraption that was destined to bring him glory or death at the hands of King Philip and the Pope.

The ossuary with a Jewish inscription inset

Chapter Five

Storms in the Mediterranean

The 'Falcon' had only sailed twenty-five sea miles when a bellow from the main mast shouted down to the poop deck that two French warships were astern and catching up fast. They had already passed the tiny coastal village of Gharb on the port side about three miles offshore. The Arabs had named the small West village simply because it was the westernmost hamlet on Gozo, if you didn't count the Blue Hole which was nothing more than a fishing dung hole. It comprised of not more than twelve grass and timber framed huts perched towards the beach, close to the rock formation that rose two hundred feet over their heads.

Roger hadn't considered that the French fleet that had been charged with cutting off his retreat and would have two separate squadrons making De Flor's escape impossible. George suggested he could set sail to outrun the French, but Roger felt the risk might be far too great, especially with the expected storm. Roger remained calm. He had been in similar situations and always managed to get through.

'Just like the needle of Jesus Christ and his camel,' he said.

George laughed at Roger's misquotation.

'You mean it's easier for a camel to enter the eye of a needle than for a rich man to enter the kingdom of God'.

'What we must make possible is for the French to search for God's needle in the middle of our haystack, or in this case, let them find God's needle in the middle of the Mediterranean.'

George ordered two lookouts to quickly go atop the main mast., one facing forward to give updates on the imminent storm and the other checking aft to give warning if the French pursuers were gaining and to what degree.

'Order each man to take a flag with them, one white and the other blue, just in case the wind noises make it harder to understand our messages. Maybe it is time to let them know what flag we should fly.'

George considered the order for a brief second before checking with his Captain if he desired the white flag with the Red Cross, or the black flag that he truly hadn't seen properly. The only time George caught a glimpse of it was in La Rochelle harbour, and on that occasion, he only had a brief view of a dark flag, hardly fluttering at night.

Roger looked on in anger at his sailing master, 'Mister Ward, we are now stateless, homeless and we ain't got too many friends left in the world. From this moment on I suggest you put away our crusader flag. From now on we fly the homeless flag of Christ.'

To take the sting out of the argument De Flor bawled out to his sailing master. 'Get an update on the two men aloft, damn you!'

George climbed about thirty feet up the rigging to make sure he didn't mishear and cupped his hands, so as to make a funnel to make his voice carry. George was careful to keep a tight hold of the ship's ropes as Mediterranean storms could easily catch any sailor. He remembered the old bedtime stories passed down through the generations concerning a whole Persian fleet that sank beneath the waves during the time they were at war with Sparta (or was it Greece?). George managed to manoeuvre his hands to cup them around both ears as he waited for the replies.

'Enemy ships less than twenty miles astern'. The second reply followed within a few minutes. 'Looks like a heavy squall with eight-foot waves steadily increasing to nine or ten, five miles ahead.'

De Flor smiled. His manner was greatly calmed as he turned to George. 'They won't catch us, George. Tell the top men to keep a watchful eye fore and aft, but I suggest we reduce sail. We don't want to get caught in the middle of a gale with too much canvas set. If my judgement is correct, we should bob about like a cork in a barrel, but if the French don't shorten canvas before the storm hits them. They will be dragged down by Neptune, the Roman God. 'Let's hope Poseidon, his Greek cousin, is close by to send them all to a permanent watery grave.'

The 'Falcon' was making steady progress even with less canvas before the wind, whereas the French pursuers retained every inch of canvas out. They were closing fast, scarcely no more than two miles astern.

De Flor wondered if his plan would still work. He needed to be past the leading edge of the storm amongst the vicious spray and howling wind before the French had a chance to decrease sails, but as far as Roger could see his nemesis was gaining fast, with fire and fury in their bellies. The leading French ship was less than half a mile astern when the 'Falcon' passed through the storm's leading edge. De Flor, noticing panic on the decks on the closest hunter's face, requested his spyglass. He took the instrument to his right eye and searched for the Captain trailing him. What he saw was a crew in total disarray, running blindly about the deck, with the top men experiencing problems taking in the canvas. He noticed the opposing Captain atop the main mast with his spyglass in hand, trying to make sense of our flag. The last thing Roger noticed was that the French ship was capsizing.

George stood alongside Roger and gently patted him on the shoulders, but Roger was not impressed. 'If that shit of a French Captain had half the sense of our recently acquired goats, his ship and his sailors would be safe. He was like a sea turtle. Once turned upside down, he was helpless with no way out, and in his haste, he broke all the rules of seamanship and his crew suffered. His ship didn't just capsize - it simply turned turtle. I sincerely hope those that followed have more sense. They should have shortened their sails and waited for the storm to blow itself out. They could have lived to fight another day, but I fear they have no sense, so you can expect more French sailors swimming with the mermaids.

'If you agree, Mister Ward, I suggest we hug the African coast until we sight Mount Tariq. That way we should be clear of the French fleet.'

George asked De Flor to repeat his orders, fearing he might have misheard. 'Keep close to the North African shore, George. I left a note at my Maltese estate explaining our next port of call would be Sardinia.

George still didn't understand, but asked just the same. 'Why tell the fucking French where we are going?' De Flor smiled and patted George atop of his bald head, 'because I enjoy telling lies to confuse our enemies.'

George sadly still didn't understand the importance of lying.

The storm lasted three days before the winds ceased and the swell abated, but in those three days and night most of the crew had emptied their stomachs. What is more, three of their goats had kept safe and well. Not surprisingly, the horizon remained clear of any mast; although the top men thought they saw a small convoy of ships going north to Sardinia.

They sailed alongside the Algerian coast, passing the harbours of Annaba and Algiers until they reached the small fishing village of Oran, situated close to the border with Morocco. To drop anchor off Oran might have been a mistake as Oran was once a Spanish/French outpost. The adjacent town of Mers el-Kebir lay at the eastern end of the bay, an Almohad naval arsenal ruled by the Moroccan Berber Màsmuda tribes from southern Morocco. Before entering the large harbour, De Flor ordered his black flag to be hoisted which caused great amusement amongst the local waterside merchants. They either thought of them as devils or sea witches, but the important point was that they allowed them to take on board fifty barrels of fresh water together with fruit, figs and various root vegetables paid for by Spanish gold coins. This would hardly be enough for the journey to Scotland so an additional stop would have to be made.

With the 'Falcon' resupplied with food and water (and three lively stinking goats in the hold), we set sail for Mount Tariq but not until George told me how the port got its name. 'It comes from an emotional expression of love towards a person, or to give a long embracing hug. Originally the word meant a pillow to lay your head on at night, but in Spanish it's AL-MOHA-DA.'

George looked perplexed, but Roger came forward with his own meaning. 'Every time the girl I love ing me, or when we are together, she always gives me some Almohad.'

Roger smiled at George blushed and walked away with the pretense of working on his cabin.

He ignored George's petulance, and sat down at his charts to judge the sailing time, which he estimated as being just short of three hundred miles. Once clear of Tariq a short northwesterly course should bring the 'Falcon' off the port of Lagos. From there, a steady five hundred mile plus northerly tack would take them up to the old Roman lighthouse at Coruña.

De Flor heard George pacing up and down inside his cabin and shouted to his friend to join him. A few minutes passed before George knocked on De Flor's door and entered Roger's spacious day cabin. George remained downcast, but it was nothing to do with making him blush earlier. He looked sour and apprehensive.

He spoke to De Flor in a quiet and factual manner. There was no sense of an argument brewing, just two friends being honest with each other, 'wine, George or a glass of ale from the bootleggers of Algeria?' De Flor sensed that he needed George to remain calm. 'I have the impression that you agree with me that we need to sail two thousand miles once we pass through Mount Tariq before reaching north-west France, including sailing through one of the fiercest and treacherous waterways known to man, The Bay of Biscay.'

George just nodded. 'This time of year I fear Biscay will not be very friendly, but my main concern is our provisions. If all goes well, we should have adequate rations, but one mishap could prove our downfall.'

De Flor looked anxious. He should have thought about the rations with greater clarity, but the excitement of the recent chase had distracted him. George suggested sailing south once clear of Mount Tariq to Rabat, a three hundred mile there and back diversion, 'unless you don't consider Tangiers to be a safe harbour for one day.'

De Flor thought long and hard about Tangiers.

'There is a Kasbah there,' George answered, 'it's located in the shadows of the old fortress.'

De Flor remained unconvinced. 'A Kasbah and a fort meant soldiers, and I don't like soldiers, certainly not today.'

George mulled over Roger's tribulations before suggesting something. 'What do you think of sending eight men ashore in the two tender boats? We could load the boats with at least three or four days of rations which should be ample.'

De Flor smiled for the first time that day and whispered to George. 'Let's do it. Pass the orders on to the men. We set sail within the hour, so set a course for Tangiers.'

Chapter Six

Martyrdom & Rescue

De Flor couldn't believe his good fortune. The passage through Mount Tariq continued without any contact being made with the enemy. Three sails were sighted on the western horizon, but the distance was judged to be too far to determine their nationality. If they were French ships, they wouldn't expect the fugitives to be heading south, assuming they had been sighted. If they were English ships, De Flor considered them to be of little consequence as the English king, Edward II, had little love for supporting the French in their quarrels regarding the remnants of the Templars. His wife was the youngest daughter of King Philip IV and Joan of Navarre, but it was common knowledge that it was purely a marriage of convenience. Edward had no love for women, for his bed was normally kept warm by his male lovers, unlike his father, Old Longshanks. You knew where you were with Longshanks, but Edward - he really was a pig in a poke.

The 'Falcon' continued sailing on her southerly course to Tangiers. The three ships they had seen earlier carried on sailing in a westerly fashion to gain entry to the Mediterranean, taking no notice of the ship sailing slowly south. The top men shouted down 'Englishmen!' This held a warm feeling in De Flor's heart, whereas George merely breathed a sigh of relief.

The Falcon arrived at the port of Tangiers just after midnight. There seemed little point in showing her true colours because the ship had a multi-national crew. There wasn't a French ship docked within Tangiers harbour, but two Italian vessels and a small vessel, not much bigger than our tender boat flew the Islamic flag, the star and crescent.

'On second thoughts Mister Ward, I think we should fly our true flag.'

George wondered why De Flor was ready to fly his gruesome flag depicting bones and skulls on a sinister evil black background. 'Well if it scares you, George, I hope it will scare our superstitious enemies.'

The following dawn heralded a glorious day. Tangiers came to life in more ways than one. The two Italian vessels were still in port discharging their cargo of all kinds of fruit, whilst the small Turkish Islamic boat was loading a cargo of human innocence and misfortune. Twelve young girls, none older than ten, were being unceremoniously herded into the small unstable boat. Three men were shouting orders at the children. The young children were like lambs to the slaughter, which is probably where they might end up - in the slaughterhouse of waterside brothels. De Flor had seen this kind of slave trade before where young girls were sold by their parents for a pittance. Girls were no good to their parents except to sell them on like excess baggage in the market, but he could never get used to it. 'This is a vile trade and one that should be stopped,' he whispered to George.

George, always headstrong, gathered his thoughts together and pointed out that they outnumbered the crew of the Turkish boat.

'Not so hasty, George, best leave it until we have our own cargo loaded and wait for that stinking rowing boat to cast off. Then I suggest we wait about an hour and relieve the three moronic jackals of their cargo before it sinks to the bottom of the Atlantic.'

With the 'Falcon' fully laden with its provisions, including a sizeable brood of young chickens, Roger went ashore to see the merchant for his bill and custom clearance. He re-boarded his ship and waited patiently until the Turks had finished their dealings with the central slave master.

Soon after midday the Turks cast off and slowly rowed north. 'They're not in any hurry,' George speculated, thinking that their intention might be to rendezvous with a sea going ship further north. De Flor had already considered this to be a reasonable assumption as he knew the rowing boat with its flimsy cargo wouldn't get far the way she looked.

George butted in, 'them there shitheads ain't sailors or my mother's the Queen of England. They can't row to save their lives.' George spat into the water as a sign of proof he knew what he was talking about, which he did.

De Flor readily agreed and ordered his crew to look lively. 'We ain't going to wait an hour. In about fifteen minutes that boat will roll over and die, like everyone on board. We must be alongside her when the tragedy occurs or all will be lost, including the young girls. I'll willingly slaughter all three of those Turks, but if one of those damned girls is killed or drowned there'll be hell to play.'

George wanted to know why the slavers only wanted girls. Roger told him in no uncertain terms that sometimes they stole boys *and* girls, but it was highly probable that the crew would interfere with the girls before the boat reached Mount Tariq. I'll take gold and precious jewels, but I would never take a child from its mother and I'll cut the throat of anyone who would try to do it in front of me, so help me, God.'

With the provisions paid for, De Flor noticed that the small Turkish boat was lying athwart of the harbour entrance and getting in the way of all the fishing boats. He could see that the Turks would either smash themselves up in the harbour entrance or bob up and down like a cork killing all on board in an idiotic panicked attempt to make for the open sea. Either way they would all die.

Roger and George stood alongside each other on the poop deck watching in disbelief at the most dreadful example of seamanship either one of them had ever witnessed. Left to their own devices the boat would almost certainly capsize, due to their oars constantly clashing.

They were almost clear of the harbour breakwater when a rogue wave almost swamped the small boat. An oar split in two, and the young girls huddled together tightly in the bowels of the boat as the three men began arguing, blaming each other for the hasty decline in their fortunes.

De Flor viewed the Turks as contemptible lumps of excrement. 'Cast off, Mister Ward, or there won't be anyone left to rescue. Don't bother about the men. We'll only save the children, and I fear some are already lost'

Within ten minutes the 'Falcon' came alongside the wreckage of the small boat. De Flor scoured the water for any survivors but at first found none, then the top men shouted down that there were three survivors on the starboard side, about two hundred yards away. De Flor ran to the other side of the deck and witnessed one man and two girls thrashing their arms about in the cold water. George couldn't work out if the girls were trying to attract attention or if they were in a state of hopeless panic.

'Lower our lifeboat, Mister Ward,' De Flor shouted. He was already in the twelve-foot boat before it hit the water. De Flor did something incredibly stupid. He dived into the ocean without thinking about the consequences. In one instant he was in mid flight diving from the boat, the next he had gathered two scared and naked young girls. He tried to communicate to the children that he meant them no harm, but suddenly felt his leg being tugged from somewhere beneath him.

'Turks just don't know when it's their time to die,' he thought to himself as he kicked the bony hand away that gripped his ankle. De Flor quickly threw the girls into the boat and swam around in ever increasing circles trying to find any other survivors. He found the other Turk, face down, peering into the murky depths through white dead eyes.

De Flor wasn't bothered about saving the slavers. His compassion was focused elsewhere, since he noticed another girl not more than twenty yards away. He quickly swam and kicked out to the girl - but she had already lost her fight for life. Out of the fifteen who boarded the boat only two had survived.

Only two had survived

'God has looked down on you kindly this day!' De Flor spoke gently to the young girl. 'What country do you come from?' The girl was terrified, but, sensing De Flor didn't mean her any physical harm, informed him that she came from the Caves of Hercules just south of

Achakar. Her parents were poor and she had two sisters and one brother. To make ends meet they sold her to the slavers to be taken to Constantinople. The Turks hoped to spend their ill-gotten gains before the end of the year as an expression of hate to Christians depicted birth date of their Christ.

De Flor asked what their purpose in Constantinople was to be, but the girl didn't know. She was too naive. He guessed she and her former companions would be set to work in the Turkish brothels and doubted they would be treated with kindness. De Flor couldn't bear to look into the girl's face any longer, but he was profoundly pleased that her life from now on would be much better. He turned back and smiled into her innocent eyes. 'We are heading to Scotland, not that I expect you to know where Scotland is; so if you desire safe passage, we will take you there.' De Flor placed his right hand on his heart to accentuate his sincerity.

The girl recognised the honesty of the sign and the genuineness in his actions and answered with one word: 'Templar.'

De Flor tried to make his actions as plain as possible and replied, 'Yes.'

'Please forgive me. I should have asked your name and if you are hungry. I have lots of questions, but now is not the right time.'

The girl looked forsaken and sad, so sad that De Flor thought she might faint if too much pressure and too many questions were asked of her.

Eventually the young child told De Flor in a tearful stuttering voice that her name was Sara, and that when she married her name would change to Sarah.

Sara lifted her face. There was so much pain and sadness in those innocent young eyes. De Flor spoke even more gently than before. 'Please accept my apology for being too forceful and insensitive to your needs. I know you have just been through a horrendous situation, but I would like to know something about you and your family.'

Sara shaded her eyes from the morning sunlight. From her reactions, De Flor estimated that the girl had been kept prisoner underground for about two weeks, on rations of stale bread and sullied water.

De Flor asked what her friend's name was, the one he had rescued along with Sara.

Sara understood the question and tried to make the syllables come out in the right order. 'Her name is, KAT-AR-RING.' She apologised for her poor attempt. De Flor explained to the girl that his pronunciation would sound like a pig grunting and tried his best to mimic Sara's friend's name. His funny pronunciation of

81

Catherine brought a huge smile to Sara's face. 'You are a very funny man, Captain.'

'Where did you live before coming to Tangiers?' Sara understood what was being asked of her, but Catherine found the questions hard to follow and failed to appreciate why the Captain kept asking them.

Sara told him that she was originally from Egypt and that Catherine came from Cape Verde.

De Flor asked his final question, hoping it would not open up too many fears. 'What religion do you follow?'

Sara and Catherine backed their frail bodies against the far wall, fear of a surprise coming from behind. De Flor tried his best to tell the girls that he didn't want to upset them or cause them any harm, but everything he tried seemed to have the opposite effect. Eventually Sara burst out crying pleading with De Flor not to burn them at the stake, 'Isn't that what Christians do?'

De Flor looked around at his multi-national crew, hoping that someone would offer an answer to the girl's ridiculous question. He looked down at the two frail creatures and wondered whoever had put those chilling thoughts into their heads. It didn't take too long to find out the answer.

George walked over to De Flor and gently offered him a poster of declarations he tore from a wall outside a tavern in Tangiers stating Jacque De Molay, Grand Master of the Templars would be executed by fire on the 19th day of March.

The two girls cried inconsolably, and it was very difficult to work out what they were saying, but the message slowly became clearer. 'Why murder your greatest warrior, your greatest statesman, none now will follow his cause! We have converted to Christianity, but we fear few will follow such a great man and your leader if you burn all Christians!'

On March 19th, Jacques de Molay together with hundreds of other Templars, after enduring torture and many other humiliations, will be sent to their deaths in a Paris square. De Molay was an old man of seventy plus years, tired with life, but proud of his achievements. He knew that the tragedy which touched his brothers and himself was the result of conspiracies. De Molay was aware that King Philip IV of France had already decided to execute and torture hundreds of innocent people, including thousands of untouched virgins together with the loyal knights of France. It was rumoured De Molay with his dying words would curse everyone who conspired in his murder. No wonder the girls had second thoughts to join the ranks of the Christian faith.

De Flor needed to get to France. Unless he witnessed Molay's death with his own two eyes, he would never inwardly accept the Grand Master's death. He told George to set sail for Dover where he hoped to see him again. Meanwhile, he would disguise himself as the sole survivor of the Turkish rowing boat disaster. De Flor had some papers taken from the drowned men that could serve a useful purpose.

He quickly scooped up the documents. He was now a sailor from the 'Serpent', a ship that regularly sailed out from Izmir which was the third most populous city in Turkey, after Istanbul and Ankara. De Flor assumed that the drowned man was a crew member of this ship as she was the only Ottoman vessel waiting silently in the next bay out of sight of the 'Falcon.' The Ottoman Turks captured the city of Constantinople previously known as Byzantium. It held a unique place in history as the only city in the world that sat on two continents, namely Europe and Asia.

De Flor felt reasonably satisfied with the progress he had made to date. Eighteen Templar ships had escaped the devious clutches of the King of France and had scattered in secret locations known only to Molay and De Flor. Roger had safely repossessed an ancient relic which he placed in a battered old sea trunk, safe from prying eyes. His only regret was the capture and torture of his close friend and Grand Master of the order, Jacques De Molay. As he recalled Molay's name, a terrible thought entered his mind. With the imprisonment of Jacques De Molay and an execution within six months, the Knights Templar would be no more, erased from history like so many others that went before them. The Romans had tried unsuccessfully to eradicate Jesus Christ, the pagan Queen Boudicca and Spartacus from history. They may have all been brutally murdered by Rome, but the names of the martyrs would live on forever, whereas Rome had ceased to have its grip on the world.

History has always been written by the victor, and it followed that Rome had too many victories. One day a great general will lose and suffer an inglorious defeat and his name will be erased from Roman history books, another defeat will follow and Rome will quickly forget their glory days. If you have too many defeats or in-fighting between the various legions Rome would die. Another great powerful Empire will take over the reins. One thousand years of Rome's domination and those early illustrious statesmen will be lost to history and people's memories. All you have left will be the wasters and degenerates who have squandered Rome's power and former glories will instinctively be forgotten, as sure as night follows day. What you have left is the filth living in the gutters and the scum and bloodied blades waiting in the shadows. It is always too late to whet your blade when the trumpet blows.

Roger explained his plan to George just before sighting the 'Serpent' in the next bay. 'You will hold the 'Falcon' within this bay, I will wear the rags of one of the drowned sailors and enter the water abreast of their ship and swim out to meet it. I will tell them our small boat was capsized by a high wave, which is true, and I was the sole survivor. My two shipmates along with the slaves were all lost. If my plan works I will be united with the Serpent's crew. They have to moor somewhere in Spain or France before continuing to Turkey. I will slip ashore and make my way to Paris.'

De Flor's plan, hasty as it was, worked well. He was hauled aboard by the Turk's and given a hot meal before the Captain spoke to him. De Flor's story was readily accepted and without further ado he was immediately set back to work.

As the Serpent sailed westward through the Mediterranean, he played games with his fellow crew members, teasing them with historical questions. He tested them on Roman history, everyone knew about Rome and their generals - De Flor asked them who they thought the first Roman leader was. They all quickly shouted - Gaius Julius Caesar, he was the first emperor of Rome. They all forgot about Augustus Octavian, who *was* the first to hold that office. He was the grandnephew of Julius Caesar; followed by Tiberius then Caligula Claudius came next and of course Nero. It seemed to the Turk's that the Roman Empire, the biggest the world had ever known at that time was ruled by self-opinionated, dysfunctional madmen. For nearly nine hundred years the Roman Empire disappeared, only to be followed by other madmen. The Franks conquered northern Gaul; the Burundians took eastern Gaul, while the Vandals replaced the Romans in Hispania. The Romans were having great difficulty stopping the Saxons, Angles and Jutes overrunning Britain.

The transition period Europeans were going through at that time became known as the period of famine. The disease was to be the new master of the world and there was nothing God or any Empire could do to prevent it from spreading.

What the people failed to comprehend, but De Flor guessed to be the truth, was that a far greater deliverer of death must soon set foot in the world. Rich or poor, young or old, it didn't matter, it would affect everybody. In terms of carnage alone, no war has even come close to that level of long-term devastation. It would be more catastrophic than Rome's disintegration a millennium before, which had, in turn, we know today as The Middle Ages.

'The Grim Reaper or as he heard the Jews call him the Angel of Death,' came their collective reply. The sailors opened their mouths wide in horror as they suddenly realised that perhaps there was very little between the two and their new shipmate had somehow tricked them. De Flor suggested that many only saw what they expected to see; nothing more and nothing less. You only see what you want to see.

De Flor quickly scribbled sketched a strange drawing on a scrap of paper and asked a shipmate what he saw.

Feeling assured that his position aboard the 'Serpent' was secure; De Flor asked the men if he knew what the next port of call might be and was surprised when he heard the reply.

'Some of the crew are paying-off at Marseille. Speak with the Captain. I feel sure he will release you if you need to be somewhere in a hurry.'

De Flor had to think of something quickly when he addressed the Captain.

'It's my wife. She is expecting our first child at the beginning of March.'

The Captain probably thought the excuse was a lie, but knew he could find better crewmen in Marseille than those who wanted to drift away. 'They are just like flotsam drifting away from well paid work. Let them idle their hours drinking, whoring and pissing in the local brothels, then mark my words they will all crawl back, just like a fox, when it pisses on the ice.'

Solomon wondered what on earth De Flor was talking about, 'fox`s, ice and piss,' he said.

De Flor smiled and tried to explain the explanation. 'What happens when you take a piss on frozen ice?'

'Still don't follow,' was all Solomon could say.

'The urine steams, but to an uneducated fox he cannot tell the difference between steam and fire, the result of the illusion of fire causes the dim witted fox to run away in disarray. You are not like the fox; you have brain, although sometimes I wonder about that.'

Chapter Seven

Onwards to Paris

Once the Serpent was safely moored alongside the Quayside at Marseille the sailors who were being paid off collected their possessions and made their way to the Captain's quarters to receive their pay from the purser. De Flor wasn't interested in receiving any payment, his needs were simple, to get ashore with the other men who were being paid off. With all the comings and goings on the Serpent and on the Quayside it was relatively easy to slip ashore without being questioned.

The Turkish vessel, the 'Serpent' moored alongside the foulest jetty on Marseille's notorious Quayside on the first day of March, allowing De Flor seventeen days to reach his destination at Île de la Cité. Strictly translated as the Island in the City, which lay in the middle of the River Seine in the centre of Paris. This was where the Parisians enjoyed putting on a show of how the execute political or religious prisoners'. ???

Unbeknown to De Flor the anticipated crowd had already been provoked beyond fever pitch for the great spectacle of witnessing De Molay final breath of death by burning. De Flor reflected on his friend's fate; burning to death might be one of the worst possible ways to die. Human flesh does not catch fire easily, so burning to death can be a slow and painful process. There are a number of ways that you can die from side effects of the fire before the fire actually kills you. But until you lose consciousness, you're going to be in agony.

'When the yellow dies under the velvet thoughts Blood-bubbles nestled in thorns,' De Flor contemplated the words he had beaten into him by that first Templar ship when he was a boy of eight. *'At the gates with fear I kiss the burning darkness.'* Why he should have dark thoughts meandering within his mind Roger hadn't a clue. He hadn't previously thought too much of De Molay fate, 'death by burning was just a phrase until now,' but it had smashed into De Flor's head like a runaway cart, he had one last thought that simply wouldn't go away. De Flor decided to shield his red tear saddened eyes of the world about him, - *burn me free from your bitterness and hate.*

A horse, De Flor needed a horse. He hadn't previously set foot in Marseille until now, and if he had a choice he wished not to be within this shit hole today. The stench of fish, horse dung and stale beer made him wretch, an unusual state of affairs that De Flor was unaccustomed to. He considered the combination of the foul French air coupled with the impenitent death of his friend had hastened his vomit to repel all within his guts, but vomit he did, and felt no better for it afterwards. If De Flor had been more vigilant, he might have noticed a stranger who had taken a personal interest in what Roger De Flor was doing, or where he was going in such a hurry. However, he had been aware of another man acting suspiciously, but that was not uncommon on the waterside. Roger made a mental note of precisely what the man was wearing, although he didn't see any weapons.

De Flor strolled along the waterfront looking for the way out of the busy port; he was also on the lookout for any farrier's, at the same time he kept a sharp eye on the man that was taking a keen interest on his every movement.

There didn't seem much point wandering around Marseille attracting attention to himself. The only course of action was to ask a local for the best horse trader within the port boundaries. Money wasn't a problem with De Flor as he had won many a game of cards aboard the 'Serpent' prior to its arrival in the French port.

Three individuals recommended Gabriel's Stables which lay at the crossroads between the main exit and the church of Saint-Laurent, four hundred yards further along the quayside. A sailor told him 'you cannot miss it, just follow your nose, the horse dung will tell you when you are close.' Either his directions or his nose told him he was near to the stables, signs on the walls informed De Flor that manure was available free of charge and inviting the customer to take away as much as he could carry.

As he turned to the exit gate leading to the commercial district of Marseille De Flor witnessed a small group of well dressed French aristocrats with their man servants inspecting the hind quarters of a young filly. It seemed that the discussions surrounded the price as opposed to the mare's fitness and breeding. Eventually the group broke-up with an enormous fee being agreed.

Gabriel looked pleased with himself as he pocketed a bundle of bank notes which he carefully placed in the huge leather apron that looked way too big for the horse trader.

De Flor introduced himself, careful not to give his identity away. He enquired if the trader had any cheaper stock within his stables. Gabriel's face turned sour at the prospect of receiving a few francs, as opposed to bargaining with those who had more money than they knew what to do with it.

Eventually Gabriel led out a horse of mature age for De Flor's inspection. However, it was plain to see that De Flor was not impressed with the animal that was only fit for the slaughterhouse or the glue factory. The horse trader knew instinctively he was not dealing with a young upstart and within a few minutes he paraded out a nice four year old mare. Gabriel didn't argue about the price De Flor mentioned, and even incorporated the saddle and blanket within the price.

De Flor was happy with his powers of horse trading as he managed a grimace of a smile which quickly evaporated when he observed the young man he perceived earlier following him ambling to Gabriel's Yard. The man didn't appear troubled as De Flor's recollections flooded his memories - same robes, same head gear, and same coloured footwear.

De Flor sensed danger, but for the want of any worthwhile weapon he stood frozen to the spot, eyes wide open trying to look for a way out. He hadn't remembered seeing the stranger, he guessed to be his killer with any kind of blade, but suddenly a curved dagger was in his hand. His would be assassin was no more than an arm's length from his chest as his destroyer flipped the blade from one hand to the other in the blink of an eye, the blade came too quickly but something unexpected registered in De Flor's brain. He expected to be in agony with an assassin's blade in his heart, but that was not the sensation his brain registered. As he instinctively fell to the ground in anticipation of glimpsing the afterlife, however, his trousers might have been wet but his heart was still beating.

As he lay motionless on the straw covered stable yard De Flor mind was puzzled - surely at a distance of just three feet the hired assassin couldn't miss, but here he was alive and unscathed.

The stranger slowly bent down and offered De Flor his hand to assist his rising which he gratefully accepted.

'You are an easy person to follow Captain, surely you must remember me; I have been in your footsteps ever since we sailed past the circular fortresses of La Rochelle, I was with you at your side after we climbed the hill to your childhood home in Malta, but it appears you did not see me, you couldn't see the wood for the trees.'

'Your name,' De Flor asked with a slight tinge of tribulation.

'My name is Solomon,' was the reply. I was once a member of the infamous Sicarii, but that's a long time ago, before I realised the errors of my judgement. You might recall from your Christian Bible that Judas Iscariot was a member of the sect, but that was not true - he was just a misguided man - remember never believe all you are told.'

De Flor turned to see another man laying face down on the stable yard straw. Solomon facial expression was all that was necessary to indicate the dead man. 'He was your enemy - your assassin,' he explained. 'It is very strange how you chose me as your intended executioner and chose him as a man of little consequence, but I suppose you still have a lot to learn.'

De Flor knew when he was verbally beaten, 'I think you might be correct young Solomon.'

The commotion in Gabriel's stable yard attracted a small crowd of curious onlookers, everyone loved a fracas and the recent activities of the young Jew and De Flor certainly attracted a lively group of men like bees around the honey pot.

De Flor felt like he was being spied on by all present and became anxious to finish his horse deal. 'My man and I must make haste, get the horse ready,' De Flor ordered Gabriel. We are both needed in the capital to attend to urgent business,' Solomon turned to look at De Flor excited by the trip that up until a few minutes past he knew nothing about.

With that Gabriel saddled up the horse he had just sold, and was eternally appreciative when De Flor offered to purchase another horse for Solomon. 'You cannot keep up with me on foot as we journey to Paris,' De Flor laughed.

'We are strange bedfellows you and me, you a Jew and me a Templar, all be it a former Templar. We now fly the flag of the outcast and nationless. Today we are but a few, but tomorrow we will be many.' This time De Flor laughed uncontrollably leaving Solomon wondering if his captain was in control of his faculties.

The journey from Marseille to the outskirts of Paris took four days, four days in which the two men enjoyed each other's company and learned much from each other's culture. Solomon had many strange stories to impart, including his childhood when living at Joppa or as he called it the 'Hill of Springs,' whilst others related to the Mediterranean coastal city as meaning 'Beautiful or Beauty.'

De Flor also learnt that Joppa, or Jaffa was the foremost port of Judea exporting oranges, the town had links with the Jewish bible when King Solomon exported timber from the forests in Lebanon in the construction of his famous Temple in Jerusalem. The Greeks referred to Lebanon after the Phoenicians because of the rare, highly prized purple-indigo dye they sold.

Roger decided it best not to divulge any of his past regarding the slaughter of Jews by some of his former companions.

'Some things are best untold!'

Solomon felt very much at ease in De Flor's company, although there were times he touched on subjects that perhaps should have been left unsaid, especially the ossuary he collected from his estate in Malta. Solomon felt embarrassed about raising the matter which left De Flor suspicious and curious why Solomon brought the subject up.

Early morning on the sixth of March De Flor and Solomon approached the small settlement of Créteil which lay seven miles southeast of Paris. The cocks were noisy as they led their horses through the muddy, rutted road which led through the middle of the town as De Flor tried in vain to find a tavern or hostelry. Time was now on their side as they only had a leisurely ride to arrive in Paris, not that either man had any chance of changing history, all De Flor required was to witness the spiteful murder of Jacque de Molay. No doubt the prisoner would be well guarded and too weak to assist in any foolhardy rescue attempt, not that De Flor had any consideration on a rescue.

'Solomon, why do you wish to breach the subject of my ossuary?' De Flor asked, wondering if his Jewish friend was playing the Devil's advocate. 'It has worried me for some time if your display of companionship is truth or not.'

Solomon looked shocked at the accusation, and offered a previously unknown hand gesture to mark his sincerity. 'If you are that interested,' he retorted, 'I will willingly explain, but my reasoning might shock you.'

'First, let me explain to you the biblical parable regarding the Good Samaritan,' Solomon calmly explained his story with confidence. 'You will recall the parable is about a traveller who is stripped of clothing, beaten, and left half dead alongside the road. First a priest and then a Levite passed by, (the Levires were Priests), but both avoid the man. Finally, a Samaritan happens upon the traveler. Samaritans and Jews despised each other, but the Samaritan helps the injured man. Jesus is described as telling the parable in response to the question from a lawyer, *and who is my neighbour?'* In response, Jesus tells the parable, the conclusion of which is that the neighbour figure in the parable is the man who shows mercy to the injured man, that is the Samaritan.

'You are not of the Jewish faith, so I have doubts if you really fully understand the meaning of the parable - let me translate for you?'

'A certain man was going down from Jerusalem to Jericho, and he fell among robbers, who both stripped him and beat him, and departed, leaving him half dead. By chance a certain priest was going down that way. When he saw him, he passed by on the other side. In the same way a Levite also, when he came to the place, and saw him, passed by on the other side. But a certain Samaritan, as he travelled, came where he was. When he saw him, he was moved with compassion, came to him, and bound up his wounds, pouring on oil and wine. He set him on his own animal, and brought him to an inn, and took care of him. On the next day, when he departed, he took out two denarii, gave them to the host, and said to him, take care of him. Whatever you spend beyond that, I will repay you when I return.' Now which of these three do you consider to be my neighbour?'

'Jesus said, *He who showed mercy on him.'*

'Then Jesus said to him, *Go and do likewise.'*

Solomon continued with the parable by asking De Flor some basic questions. 'The Priest in the story is very easy to understand, however the Levite might be harder for you to understand, a Levite was a member of the Hebrew tribe of Levi, especially of that part of it which provided assistants to the priests in the worship within the Jewish temple.'

The Samaritan religion, also known as Samaritanism, is the national religion of the Samaritans. The Samaritans adhere to the Samaritan Torah, which they believe is the original, unchanged Torah, as opposed to the Torah used by Jews, hence constant conflict.

De Flor looked at Solomon showing understanding that previously had passed him by.

Solomon then told De Flor another story, one close to his heart.

'When I was a young boy I entered a Christian temple, dared by my friends, I quietly walked up the main pathway leading to a beautiful alter and gazed up at a golden statue of a man nailed to a cross.'

De Flor nodded his head to show he was following Solomon's words.

'When I was directly in front of the covered alter I looked upon the statue and was mesmerised and transfixed by its beauty; then I heard shouting from behind me calling out - *'get out Jew'*.

'This was followed by a stone which was thrown at me, catching me unaware on the back of my shoulder accompanied by the words - *'get out Jew, you are not wanted here.'*

'Before I had the chance to withdraw another stone was thrown, which missed me, but chipped the edge of the statue, with the cry of men shouting - how many times do we have to warn you - *'get out Jew, you are not welcome at our place of worship.'*

I turned around to look at the angry people behind me, before turning back to study the statue I said, *'I am not sure if they are talking to you or me but it appears we are both unwelcome from this place of worship.'*

'The morals of my parable are that the ignorant mob order me out of the temple but were happy to worship another Jew, a person they don't really know, since they called him Jesus which is simply nothing more than a Greek translation of his true name. Jesus is not a Jewish name; his correct name was **YehesHUaH** and is derived from the highlighted letters YHVH with the Jewish letter SHIN inserted in the centre creating as derived from the Christian name of Joshua. How do you expect to understand the plight of the Jews when you don't even know to the Messiah's name, so whom is my neighbour?'

De Flor was silent for some minutes trying to take in everything Solomon had tried to explain. Finally he asked Solomon, 'but what has this to do with the ossuary?'

'Everything and nothing,' Solomon replied, 'when I witnessed your new flag flying aboard The Falcon I thought you had at last come to your Christian senses appertaining to the true meaning of the cross but it appears you just stumbled upon an idea without thinking too much about it.

'I will explain, but not until the time is right.'

De Flor considered himself chastised, but upon hearing Solomon's judgement he had to at least show a degree of courtesy and would be patient until his friend decreed the time would be right.

The Good Samaritan

Chapter Eight

The Green Man

The Pope had abolished the Templar movement by Papal decree two years ago, and although Molay's show-trial had been a lengthy drawn out affair the King of France ordered his body be transported from Vienne to Paris and on a rostrum erected on the parvis before the great cathedral of Notre-Dame he would publicly condemn Molay to a perpetual imprisonment. De Flor knew that Molay would loudly profess his innocence and that of all Templars. A commission of three cardinals under the King's authority would condemn Molay and other dignitaries of the order to perpetual imprisonment.

On hearing his sentence, Molay again retracted his confession, and as a final punishment the King sentenced the Templars Grand Master to death by burning as a relapsed heretic. The King's officers were ordered to inflict the sentence on an island in the River Seine in Paris on the grounds of public safety; however, it was thought that the King wanted any verbal remarks to be kept out of vision and earshot of the crowd.

That was not the full story; the inhabitants of Paris, on the intended day of execution, would be swelled by a large crowd of bewildered onlookers within the surrounding districts, wondering if De Molay would curse the dark souls of the Pope and King.

The Templars had always been considered the Fighting Monks arm of the period, the Soldiers of Christ or the pious protectors of Christian Pilgrims from any unprovoked attacks from bandits and non-Christians, but by a show of strength by the French King he ordered his trusted royal guard to keep the majority of the gathering far away from the intended place of execution, with the intention of muting and obscuring the crowds vision.

With temporary lodgings, having been secured in Créteil, Solomon and De Flor rested in their room until the sun-set in the late afternoon. Both men found peace in each other's company and wondered if it would ever be possible to solve the ancient problem of co-existence within the three major religions.

Solomon doubted if a lasting peace would ever be achievable in Europe or the Holy Land, but De Flor brought up an interesting piece of evidence which Solomon had not previously known. According to Roger De Flor a symbolic peace was contrived in the Iberian

Peninsula between the Christian Hispania, Jewish Sefarad, and Islamic al-Andalus. The aim of the religious peace treaty was to try to understand the numerous conflicts within communities as well, such as the tensions between Christian Arian Visigoths and native Catholic Iberians and the fundamentalist North African Almohad Dynasty. They explored the unique role of the Jewish community who Muslims and Christians depended upon as political and cultural intermediaries as well as their intellectual collaborators, however, as the principle antagonists were the Spanish Christians after the conquest the Muslim conquest of the peninsular. They tried to trace and explore the origins and trajectory of conflict between these two great religious communities. The pivotal point appeared to be the Muslim conquest of Spain, which blocked Christian Reconquista, prohibiting the intermixing of peoples, and expulsions, which they termed as ethnic cleansing - whatever that means. De Flor knew what this cleansing was about but was unable to find a less harsh meaning to describe the tragedy of Iberia during the troublesome period which had festered during the past five hundred years. It was hoped to pacify the two religions by introducing the Jews into the mixing pot. De Flor continued with his knowledge of Islamic Spain, 'it is sometimes described as the *'golden age'* of religious and ethnic tolerance and interfaith harmony between Muslims, Christians and Jews.'

De Flor finished his narrative by adding the words, 'we are but mortal men so power corrupts, but absolute power corrupts absolutely. If left in the hands of the hierarchy every group wanted more power than their destined entitlement. The harmony of men should be left to mere men alone. Political and Religious leaders should never be trusted with the hearts of men; they can rule their own specific destiny by the power of their individual beating hearts.'

Solomon looked on expressionless as though he was lost in his forests of Lebanon, which to an extent he was. He hadn't understood a word of which De Flor had said.

De Flor was anxious to return to the matter of the Jewish ossuary box, together with Solomon's remarks about *the true meaning* and *Christian senses*. Should he take these words as being something to be taken literally or was this another Samaritan riddle.

Solomon remained steadfast in not divulging any additional information until his Christian friend had come to his senses. What should he take from these two remarks, what was he missing. De Flor was tempted to ask Solomon directly, but he didn't want to appear ignorant of the inner truth that he should have known but failed to comprehend the obvious.

Instead De Flor settled for a stalemate in the stupid riddles. 'Let's get the mounts ready and explore our road ahead on the final leg journey to Paris.'

Solomon willingly complied; he was getting fed up with De Flor's ignorance.

The pair left the town shortly after sunset and arrived on the outskirts of Paris two hours later. The two men had not been alarmed by anything on the road they travelled, they had not been challenged by any soldiers. This could mean the King was over confident or he had not considered any rescue attempt for De Molay.

That damn fox and pissing on ice came to both men's minds. There was no rescue plan; they were in Paris to confirm what heinous preparations King Philip IV and the Pope Clement had in mind, and to hear with their own ears what De Molay had to say during his final breaths on God's earth. Whatever the men had in mind would not be pleasant but brutal. Solomon muttered, 'brutality needs to be matched with brutality,' but De Flor reminded his travelling companion that there would be time at sometime in the future for God to intervene, 'what goes around, comes around.'

The symbolic wood carving of 'The Green Man.'

The first tavern the two friends came across was called *'L'homme vert'* or as translated into English 'The Green Man.' They quickly tied their horses to the posts outside the tavern and walked through into the noisy bar. Solomon hadn't seen the effigy of the Green Man figurine prior to walking into the tavern, but as soon as he turned to amble past the wood carving he appeared visibly shocked and upset as if the sign led to gloom, obscurity and evil. No such sign was noticeable within his native forest of Lebanon. De Flor, quickly noticing his friend's distress tried to put him at ease, but it took a few minutes to get him into the crowded interior of the tavern. The majority of the customers were vehemently agitated in the forthcoming executions, whilst others were trying to avoid the heated discussions which normally led to brawling by those playing cards - everything and anything to evade to debate.

The absence of soldiers in the vicinity probably meant these peasants were full of wind and vinegar, the latter is usually taken to mean empty talk, full of bombast; vinegar, in this case being associated with the sourness and acidity.

Solomon, still visibly shocked by his recent ordeal thought the expression was full of wind and piss, but De Flor corrected him by explaining, 'vinegar has a terrible taste compared with piss, so in France piss it is.'

The two men settled down to two pints of watered down French ale, Solomon nearly spat out the contents within his filled mouth after sampling his first mouthful - 'this tastes like piss he loudly shouted proclaimed, which brought hales of laughter with a few looks of horror from the customers at the immediate tables, or maybe it's vinegar, he corrected himself, which brought rounds of unexpected laughter. Solomon and De Flor both laughed at the escape that could have easily brought physical disaster from the wrath of the landlord.

'From now on listen and don't talk,' De Flor whispered to his Jewish friend - you have two ears and only one mouth, so you will hear twice as much as you will ever speak.'

Solomon considered the proverb and quickly agreed with its sentiment and quickly understood that the Crown and Church were acting very much against the feelings of the people. 'Believe me,' Solomon retorted, 'I know as I used to be the number one culprit. For a very long time all I did was talk. I somehow felt the need to talk as much as possible. I used to take very quick breaths so I could continue speaking before anyone tried to interrupt me. Now that I am armed with this fundamental information I will learn to hold my peace and from now on I will carefully listen to all I hear.'

De Flor felt proud of himself; at last he had taught his friend an important way of gathering information.

The two men spent a pleasant, if not noisy, evening within the Green Man tavern, but all they really learnt was that the people mainly supported the Templars against the Church and the King. De Flor considered his statement concerning wind and vinegar and settled on the opinion that what he was hearing was an extreme form of empty talk, and most certainly full of bombast. What surprised the two friends was the absence of soldiers or spies, they normally stuck out like sore thumbs, however this evening within the tavern people

114

seemed to talk freely of revolt and rebellion - when the peasant population spoke in terms of insurrection you knew excessive drink was the likely cause, either that or swank.

Solomon appeared nervous and asked of his captain if they should retire to their lodgings before the braggers got completely out of hand to attract attention from the local authorities, De Flor wasn't truly bothered, he could handle himself and keep out of trouble, but he had never seen his friend forced to defend himself and agreed with his Jewish companion - so back the rest and sleep - 'a busy day tomorrow,' Solomon related.

De Flor added, 'we will have to be extremely cautious until this horrendous chapter in my life is over.'

Solomon looked at his captain to tell him that whatever tribulations and dangers he had to face, he would not face them alone - 'we are united in our faith in the service of one God, for I believe my God and yours are known to each other, but no related, we can add the God of Mohamed to this threefold relationship - they are one and the same. It must therefore follow that the three major religions are all bound by a special sacred bond.'

De Flor found Solomon's initial line of reasoning hard to follow at first, but after thinking about it for a brief period of time he nodded his agreement and fully understood the simple logic behind his claim.

'If we are bound to God,' Solomon continued, 'by a sacred bond, why do we fight each other?'

De Flor quickly interrupted, 'because, I suspect it's easier to fight than to love.'

This was turning into a game of out brinkmanship between the two friends as Solomon tried to get the last phrase into the debate, 'but remember my friend, it is always easier to fight for one's principles than to live up to them.'

Not to be out done De Flor countered by expressing his willingness to give up fighting to be an ambassador for peace. 'I have fought all my life, most of the time in honourable combat and sometimes by deception and trickery. I will live out my remaining days living up to the principles of peace and understanding.'

Solomon was shocked, a man of war taking up the challenge of peace, 'but what if you are confronted by evil?'

'Then that will be the time for talking,' was De Flor's response. 'I am getting old my friend, my fighting arm hurts, it grows weaker as the weeks go by; so do you expect me to fight all my life. I have been fighting since I was eight years of age - enough is enough. De Flor wondered what his friend Ramon would make of his enlightenment. 'Once I was lost in the darkness, but now I have seen the light.'

'I expect you to fight for God, as he fights for you every year of your life.' Solomon raised his head to the heavens as if he was looking for a sign - but none came. 'Nothing now remains but to offer you an inkling of what you have to unravel for yourself, why did you wear the sign of the cross on your mantel and shield, what was its purpose, and if your answer be nothing, then never wear it again. The cross has no relevance in Christianity.

De Flor was greatly alarmed; was Solomon offers him another Jewish riddle from his companion, or was he trying to confuse him, no relevance in Christianity - that's plain bullshit. Whatever the answer, he couldn't give a quick reply as Solomon had already removed himself from the room.

A Knight Templar

De Flor never understood the part money played with the Templars. Obviously some had money, some had heaps of money, but he just got by on his reserves from mercenary contracts and acquired loo all of which had of course dried up within the past years. He had attempted to live under the Templars code of being a poor Knight of Christ

One explanation that the token or seal device is that it was originally intended to commemorate the poverty of the Order, which could only afford one horse for each pair of Knights or if a knight had his horse killed from under him another knight would rescue him from the battlefield. However, both these explanations are hotly contested, especially when you consider the written Statutes of the Order which expressly enjoined that each Knight would be provided with three horses. Even the *'frater's servientes armiger'*, or men-at-arms, of whom a body attended each Knight, were each allotted one horse, however De Flor thought the best explanation of the seal was that it displayed the dual roles of the Knights, however they being warrior monks, they were poor but grew to be the richest organisation of its time. They were devoted to Jesus Christ, but vert of the awareness of the commercial life necessary to their existence.

De Flor only had the one horse, and he was forced to purchase that in Marseille, he had to buy a second horse for Solomon. He suddenly sat bolt upright. 'Bloody hell, I forgot to water and feed the damn horses.'

The famous seal of the Knights Templar

Chapter Nine

Their Final days

With the horses well rested, De Flor and Solomon rode out from the small town of Créteil back to the filth and grime of Paris. The rutted road was relatively empty save for the poor peasant's soles seeking a day's work in the French capital. Not that much work could be found; the entire country was on high alert due to the constant bickering between the English King Edward III and, Philip IV the King of France and Navarre was only young at the time, born in Fontainebleau, France in 1268. Everybody knew Philip's constant bickering with England would escalate into yet another European conflict, but the war needed to be financed and the treasury was nearly empty of gold unable to finance a new conflict with their old enemy - The English.

France owed the Templar Bank vast sums of money making it near impossible to increase the debts to finance another conflict. Hence, to fill the treasury it would be necessary for the King to increase taxation which the people would rebel against.

Philip ruled jointly with his wife, Joan I of Navarre. He had long struggled with the Roman papacy which ended with the transfer of the Curia to Avignon, France beginning with the so-called Babylonian Captivity in 1309. Philip secured French royal power by wars against the barons and his neighbours and by restriction of feudal usages.

The country would slowly degenerate into a period of artificially inflated prices for farm produce, but any future increase in taxes would be vehemently disputed by the populace.

It was in this period of gloom and anxiety that De Flor and Solomon returned to the French capital. They again decided to rest at the Green Man to keep up with the gossip and quench their dusty throats with a glass of ale and some stale bread and cheese. Before arriving at the tavern Solomon noticed six horses tethered to the wooden handrail outside. Solomon suggested it would be prudent to leave the horses at the stables and approach the Green Man on foot, let's appear as we look - poor and penniless. The friends entered the tavern and walked slowly, as if bored, to the counter and ordered two prints of ale and some scraps of food. Both of them were aware of eyes burning into the back of their necks, however, they refused to turn their heads - 'just act normal,' De Flor whispered.

'Where do you hail from strangers,' the leader of the group suddenly asked. 'Not seen you two about.'

De Flor did the talking, leaving Solomon to drink and eat. 'We are from the sailing community, paid off at Marseille and on our way to the channel ports to seek further work.'

'What ship,' asked another man?

'The Serpent, on passage from Tangiers to Turkey,' De Flor replied.

'Cargo,' a third man demanded to know.

'Cargo,' De Flor replied, not much cargo, mainly fruit I think, the holds were sealed due to the high winds off Mount Tariq.'

The third man carried on with his questions, 'I heard the ship carried a number of slaves.'

'Yes, bound for somewhere in Turkey, but as I said, we paid off at Marseille, didn't fancy Turkish food.' This answer not proving satisfactory De Flor continued with his statement. 'There were a number of young girls who were supposed to board at Tangiers, but they all drowned together with three seamen when they tried to board The 'Serpent' whilst at anchor.'

'Yes, I heard about that, nasty business for those poor sailors drowning in the Atlantic,' the third inquisitor seemed content that his questions matched De Flor's answers, but De Flor was furious that his questioner had felt no sympathy for the young black girls, 'what about the children who drowned?'

'They are of no consequence to me, they are just girls, and black to boot, they wouldn't have lasted too long in a Turkish brothel.'

'They were just children, and they are of consequence to me,' De Flor shouted back.

Solomon realising that De Flor was getting on his high horse, whispered to him to forget it, 'let the bastard's leave, you have pledged yourself to peace and talk. You have tried to talk so leave it.'

The argument finished when the soldiers left, leaving De Flor and Solomon alone in the tavern with the exception of the barmaid. De Flor was still fuming as the men left; he sipped his ale, out of the way in a darkened corner of the tavern. 'He wants to be left alone,

Solomon explained to the barmaid; leave him alone, he'll be okay soon'

Solomon spoke to the barmaid at length, gaining information on security and troop movements within Paris. There did seem to be some sympathy for the King due to the unexpected demise of his wife whilst in childbirth, although it was rumoured that the death might have been contrived; some considered his bizarre and eccentric lifestyle was of a direct result of his being a widower so early in life. Queen Joan had not even celebrated her thirtieth birthday when she died.

The barmaid heard that the burning of Jacque de Molay would take place on Tuesday the nineteenth day of March. Agreement had been reached to carry out the execution at The Île de la Cité, principally to stave off the expected crowd. Numerous cavalry squadrons had been moved onto the island, together with the Royal Guard. If De Flor and Solomon wanted to gain access to the island they would need to be stationed there at least four days and remain well hidden with provisions; not an easy task to perform with the continual changing of the guards and continuous searching's of high buildings and church spires. Solomon imparted the information to De Flor, explaining the difficulties both men would face. De Flor looked grim, recognising the hardship they both had to experience, but for the sake of De Molay it had to be done to report back to the new Grand Master, if there was to be one, especially as the Pope had decreed the end of the Templars.

Throughout the days that followed the two men gathered all they needed for the four days required to be in hiding. Besides food and water they had to overcome the problem of human waste. Solomon suggested their hiding place should be underground, thereby making it easier to get rid of their body waste and urine, but De Flor thought the risk too high, especially when you think about the offending stench. 'No, we must be high looking down on their murderous activities,' De Flor demanded.

'So be it,' responded Solomon, 'we are in agreement.'

Finally the day to walk onto the island arrived. They both carried small bags filled with the basic provisions that were needed. They both carried a well concealed blade in case they would be discovered. De Flor put his principles to one side, although he promised to be peaceful after the burning. The first two days went by without incident; they had found a good high place to hide where they could look down on the proceedings, both men dreaded to witness, however on the third day after suffering the greatest privations and fatigue both men felt unable to continue. 'Willpower,' De Flor murmured, 'willpower and faith will see us through.' On the morning of the fourth day they were woken by much pomp and ceremony, trumpets played and drums rolled as if the day forecasted a spring holiday, but as the scene unraveled it was clear today was no holiday.

The stakes had been driven into the ground each surrounded by bundles upon bundle of fagots tied together. It was clear by the amount of fagot bundles that the night sky would remain light all night long. De Flor looked down on the congregation of dignitaries, they were all happy and smiling, especially the hundreds of Catholic priests in attendance. Seats had been arranged for the King's household, Philip himself was not there, just like the cunning Pope but other worthy fat-arsed and fat-pursed bigwigs were there, comfortable on their plump cushions during the burnings. De Flora wondered how anyone could feel pleased and satisfied with themselves at watching such a horrific barbaric act. Solomon told him, 'some have paid much gold to sit as close to the victims as possible.'

Then silence a sustained but brief silence that seemed to last an eternity until those damn trumpets sounded again. The prisoners were pushed out in single file and chained to their respective stakes as if a game was about to commence, but this was no game, unless you call *'the dance of death'* a game. Philip had previously burnt fifty-four Templars at the stake four years earlier, his acceptance of killing by fire was now well established, although Philip was not on the island,

and De Flor recognised him on the balcony of his palace sitting next to the smiling Pope.

This was Philip's greatest act of revulsion. The area was well managed with soldiers and troopers guarding the burning circle. De Flor and Solomon were still some distance away, but they heard the screams of the victims as their body fat fuelled the repugnant scene, Solomon pointed down at soldiers vomiting in horror at the noise and smell of burning flesh. It was normal at such burnings to have a rope or chain tied around the victim's neck to hasten the sufferers to a more speedy death, but none were visible on that day.

De Molay was an old man when he died, tired with life and proud of his achievements. He knew that the tragedy which touched his brothers and himself was the result of schemes. He was also aware that the King of France had decided to torture and finally executes the innocent Knights Templar - the loyal knights of France. Thus, when De Molay was dying, he cursed everyone who recommended his murder. After seven long years, Jacques de Molay ended the daily pain of tortures and the Cardinals agreed upon the death sentence for him. De Flor and Solomon witnessed the execution, and swore on oath that De Molay showed no sign of fear, and tried not to show pain during his slow death on the burning stake.

Most of the pyres were prepared in such a way that the victims would die quickly. However, in the case of De Molay, they prepared a pyre which would burn slowly. Before he died, he made his voice heard loudly once more. The results of the speech may have led the King and the Cardinals to regret not allowing him to die within a few minutes, like the other Knights.

Out of the flames which licked around him, Molay's voice was heard cursing King Philip and his family along with Pope Clement. As he experienced the agony of being burned alive; Molay is said to have invoked a 'curse' calling on Christ to prove the Order's innocence and bring its persecutors to the judgement of God.

De Flor imagined what the Templars were feeling in their hearts when the fires were lit, The effects of exposure to extreme heat, has a long history as being a form of capital punishment, and many societies have employed it for activities considered criminal such as treason, rebellious actions by slaves, heresy, witchcraft, and arson.

When people were executed by being burned at the stake, they could die from a form of smoke poisoning before the flames caused seriously damage to the body. This only happens in large fires, where multiple people were executed at once, and today there were over fifty Templars for the King to rid himself from.

The fire would first burn and peel away the thin outer layer of skin and after five minutes under the flame the thicker layer of skin shrinks and split open, and fat would begin to leak out. If you're lucky you would already be dead at this point, although the eyes would have finally bulged and explode, spewing out blood to leave gaping holes where the eyes once looked out on their persecutors.

The most severe burns cause so much damage to your nervous system that you are no longer able to feel pain. However, it's uncertain whether you would be able to survive long enough to recognize that you cannot feel pain anymore. De Flor and Solomon trusted that the creator had rendered all the knights impervious to pain, but by the cries from the middle of the fire it appeared that pain was very much causing extreme agony.

How could any man inflict such a punishment on his fellow man? De Flor was furious, how could Philip and the French Pope inflict such a death on those he once called friend?

The burning of Jacque De Molay 19th March 1314

Thus, on a dull Tuesday morning in March 1314 the institution of the Order of the Knights Templar was destroyed, dying as it was borne and lived in blood, rage and Catholic piety. It had not been destroyed completely for De Flor had the skill and foresight to sail away from La Rochelle harbour to unknown destinations. Ramon Muntaner the Templar and Chronicler, Roger De Flor the fleet captain, George Ward the Englishman left faithfully to protect the Falcon and Solomon the Jew all knew the truth about the burnings and the myths surrounding the partial demise of the Knight Templars.

Tuesday the nineteenth day of March 1314 might have been the date of the execution of our Grand Master together with hundreds of fellow Templar knights, but not the complete termination of the Templar society. De Flor and Solomon had to remove themselves from the island, retreat back to mainland Paris and make their way to a channel port and escape this vile country before meeting up with George Ward aboard the Falcon.

To distract his thoughts from the deadly burning De Flor tried to fix his mind on solving Solomon's ridiculous riddle - but he had other trials to overcome. What he had just witnessed would remain etched in his heart and soul until it was his turn and time to meet his maker.

The crowd below was shouting and cheering, it took all of Solomon's strength to restrain his friend. 'Be quiet or you will give our hiding place away,' Solomon was feeling physically sick as he tried to grab De Flor's arms, 'don't be a fool,' he cried.

He recalled the curse De Molay directed up and placed on the very souls of the respective families who had betrayed their country and their protectors. Both Solomon and De Flor prayed the curse would come about; for if it did transpire there wouldn't be any requirement for either of them to take up arms on behalf of De Molay. Hopefully the curse itself would leave both families in a state of panic, whereas Solomon trusted the two men had already filled their undergarments with their foul crap all by themselves in fear of the unknown and what was to come.

Chapter Ten

The Channel

De Flor and Solomon waited a further two days concealed on the small island in the middle of the Seine before they considered it was safe to move out of hiding. Once on the stained cobbles the pair walked together through the deserted central square where the burnings took place. The authorities hadn't bothered to clean up the desolate area where the stakes had only two days ago been driven into the ground in a large uninterrupted circle. The only evidence to mark the place of death was the filthy brown and white ash being blown by the wind and the charcoaled mess strewn haphazardly about the cobbles. The chains that bound De Molay and by which his loyal knights were restrained, lay in heaps about the disorganized stoned square. The scene of utter devastation had been left untouched to act as a reminder to others not to challenge the authority of the Crown or Church.

De Flor had often witnessed with his own eyes the carnage left behind on the battlefield as he viewed the charred and lifeless bodies of the defeated. The wounded already had their throats cut, leaving the bodies in contorted and unnatural formation; but the scene spread out before him was very different. Good loyal men, the free sons of France who would have gladly given their lives to protect their King and Country, but the King had all but annihilated his loyal men of France and cast them out from their beloved homeland, their France.

As tough as De Flor and Solomon were, both men had tears in their eyes and anger in their bellies. How could France justify their slaughter? In some way the King and the Pope had to pay for their crimes against the noble fraternity of Templars, whom had once been the pride of France, but no more, they were cast aside to the four cardinal winds of heaven never again to protect pilgrims venturing out into the blood saturated sand of Jerusalem. They had protected the pilgrims from certain death whilst travelling to the Holy Land. 'The people did nothing to stop this carnage,' De Flor shouted with contempt at those who had boasted their allegiance and protection for the Templars.

'Don't be too hard on them my friend,' Solomon replied, 'they are not trained soldiers and would have been cut down like dogs in an attempt to show their loyalty to the order.

People say many things when their bladders are full with ale or wine, but once the sun rises in the east, which you cannot hold back, their fervour disappears like snow in the springtime. Their sober heads suddenly remember where their priorities lay, the need to protect what they love - their homes, their wives and their children, all else had to be forgotten.'

De Flor acknowledged that Solomon was right, how could the unarmed and untrained labourers rise up against the odds. 'One day the French people will rise up against tyranny and oppression, and when that day comes the whole world will sit up and take notice. It might not happen in our lifetime, but as sure as eggs are eggs my prophecy will come true.

Checking the area below, completely void of men Solomon suggested they should remove themselves from the blackened landscape; reminding De Flor that the longer they lingered close to this circle of death the likelihood of recognition and arrest would be heightened. 'I don't know about you skipper,' Solomon reminded his senior, 'but I don't fancy witnessing the interior of a French dungeon. I have already felt the heat and the smell of roasting flesh to last many lifetimes.'

The two friends departed the island side by side to collect their mounts; both men took one final glance back at the horrific sight that had tarnished their minds forever. 'I don't know about you Jew, but I need a bath.'

Solomon nodded his agreement, but warned against returning to their lodgings, 'a bath in the next river will have to do.'

The two friends rested awhile on the banks of the Deûle River, which ran through the centre of the town of Lille. The weather had been unseasonably kind to them on their way back to the English Channel. They had bathed naked soon after sunset, but their clothing was of great concern, how to get it dry prior to continuing their journey. The only thought that came to mind was to steal clothing from washing lines and be off before the cock crowed to mark the renewal of another drab day. The gloom and doom felt in both men's hearts hadn't subsided during the dreary three days ride from Paris to Lille, but it had allowed De Flor time to think. Much of the journey had been spent in silence, neither man having the need to converse with the other. There had been a strange silence lurking on every track and road in France, the farm workers had all but vanished from their labours. It was if the country had not woken from a gigantic orgy of drink.

'What about Flanders,' Solomon asked De Flor, 'should we slip over the border into the Flanders and make our way towards Dunkirk,' he continued.

'Call yourself a sailor - Dunkirk is in France you idiot,' De Flor retorted, 'but yes, I agree Flanders, or perhaps another quiet backwater in France would be more suitable.' De Flor thought about the situation and after deliberation suggested, 'the fishing port of Grand-Fort-Philippe. The port would be the ideal place to obtain safe passage back to English waters and a welcome reunion with the *'Falcon'* and Mister Ward. Many of the fisher folk were renowned for the smuggling activities. 'There isn't a harbour or river there as such, but it has a man-made canal, making it a good location ideal for our needs,'

The two men reached the small hamlet of Le Clair Marais on the outskirts of the fishing port of Grand-Fort-Philippe soon after midnight. The need for rest outweighed the need for urgency. The two men slept within a small wooded area directly south of the hamlet. De Flor advocated caution, suggesting they should proceed with vigilance; 'we have to ensure the pathway leading to the port is free of guards. We have to ascertain if the path is clear of soldiers who might be billeted in the vicinity or if any soldiers were based within the small port,' but first they had to release the horses', or sell them.

139

Solomon informed De Flor that he had sighted a small farm to the west that appeared to be horse free. 'I would much prefer to donate the horses to the farmer than to release them.'

'I have no objections to your noble sentiments my friend,' De Flor cheerfully replied. 'I have been trying to empty my head of those dreadful images we witnessed in Paris by thinking about your riddle. You explained to me that the cross had no place in Christianity; I find that hard to believe. I know the sign of the fish has relevance in our religion, but at first I couldn't understand that the cross had no significance, but then it suddenly occurred to me that the only mention of the cross was the instrument by which our Lord was crucified. Am I correct thus far?'

'The Roman's must have crucified thousands of victims; I have further noticed the lack of an abundance of trees in Jerusalem. The Roman's were notorious for their building work and would have calculated the design of their creation of death so as to preserve the supply of as much timber as possible - nothing was wasted. In my extensive travels I have witnessed many sights of execution and most have a simple stake driven into the ground, sometimes it could be the remnants of a tree, I have seen a few with a crossbar device, but seldom seen a cross as depicted in the Christian books - am I on the right track,' De Flor asked more out of anticipation than a question.

Solomon nodded and remained silent; he wanted to know how much De Flor had found out for himself.

'I have even seen paintings of saints being crucified upside down, but I never understood the reasoning behind it. However the 'Tau' formation or a single stake seems the most likely. I feel certain in my own mind that the *'Tau cross'* set in the form of the letter 'T' would be the preferred design used by the Roman's. If I am right the *'Christian cross'* is wholly inaccurate, whereas the *'tau cross'* was adopted by the first Christians, as its shape reminded them of the cross on which Christ was crucified'.

The Crucifixion by Anthony van Dyck.
depicting the Virgin Mary, St John and St Mary Magdalene.

De Flor looked smug for the first time in a week; he had witnessed so many atrocities in his life he was now determined to promote peace, but to live up to this principle was much harder than he envisaged.

Solomon laughed out loud and slapped his friend on the back as a mark of his understanding of past errors.

Crucifixion was performed in many ways, and the Romans of old were especially adept at it. But generally each variation would fall into one of those two categories. The slow method would very often involve nailing the victim's wrists to the patibulum, or crossbeam. Their feet would be nailed, either separately, or together, one atop the other, onto the stauros, or upright stake. In addition, their arms would be tied with ropes. Most of the time a horn or protrusion would be affixed to the stauros, at the level of the victim's groin and the body weight could be rested upon it. The victim's blood would quickly coagulate and they would remain in this position for days. Their death was often from thirst or exposure, but normally from sometimes sheer exhaustion.

De Flor was the Count of Malta, and the Maltese flag was designed around the Christian cross, although the Maltese cross had four equal in length sides, unlike the cross of Christ. 'I have not mentioned the most brutal crucifixion, that of a single stake, or the one which the sufferer was left for hours in unqualified agony. The Roman's did dream up hellish ways to kill anyone who stood against them. So if there is confusion regarding the Templars crosses, the depiction of a cross must originate from somewhere.'

'True,' answered Solomon, 'and you have the proof where it originated.'

De Flor felt uneasy; Solomon thought the transgression from Roger's calculations to the reality of the cross would be easy, but De Flor was unable to visualise the final piece of the puzzle.

Unless the final piece of the puzzle was connected with the crossed bones within the ossuary box, the femur bones could only fit diagonally with the skull delicately positioned atop the femur's inside the box.

'Eureka, you have it,' Solomon was impressed with De Flor's calculations, 'if the cross was designed in the form of an 'x' it wouldn't have been so much of a problem, however your ossuary box is extremely unique, there is nothing like it in the world.'

'Before the pair of us get over excited about the contents of your ossuary box we have to get inside the fishing port unseen, make it financially worthwhile for the skipper to smuggle us across the channel before we can shake George's hand again.' Solomon hoped the exercise was simple enough not to go wrong. The French had long called the channel as the moat protecting England from invasion. 'If we forget about William the Bastard and Gaius Julius Caesar, the moat around our coast has done its job well,' Solomon explained.

'Shall we check if our plan is feasible?' De Flor was excited, he felt confident that within a day or two they both would be standing on the deck of the Falcon with George, but Solomon was yet to be convinced, remember our chain is only as strong as its weakest link. De Flor remarked, 'there is no weak link, nothing can go wrong as long as we are careful.'

Solomon and De Flor ambled towards the path leading to the port area; there didn't seem any security guarding the gate, however, as soon as the two men stepped through the gate, they were confronted by four soldiers who demanded to know their intentions and where they were going. Solomon stuttered by replying they were common sailors looking for work, however, it was not surprising that his answer didn't impress the sergeant in charge. 'We are here to challenge everybody attempting to leave France, he shouted. Solomon thought the man's clean stripes had gone to his head. 'There ain't any skippers aboard their craft - the port is closed on the orders of the Crown.'

'Why should the Crown close the port,' De Flor queried.

'On account of any traitors escaping by means of stealing our boats,' the sergeant replied, 'only yesterday we apprehended two men who it turns out to be escaping Templars. We strangled the life out of them this very morning.'

'So you think we look like Templars,' Solomon in anger shouted at them, 'we couldn't hold a sword if we tried, we ain't had any training,' De Flor added.

'Whether you like it or not, we have no choice but to secure you for questioning and if the officer decrees you are sailors he might convey you to the press gang holding point where the King is in need of good seafaring men, otherwise we have enough bullets left to practice our shooting skills tomorrow morning.'

The two men were unceremoniously manhandled to a small hut to the rear of a boat repair yard, timber was stacked high ready to replace planks shot through in previous engagements. Fires were burning in small braziers ready for caulking with wool and tar. 'You can have a mug of beer and some cheese if you want,' the sergeant bellowed before waiting for a reply. Two dirty mugs, half filled with the worst beer De Flor had ever tasted were pushed through a large crack between the uprights of the hut and into the room, together with two minute lumps of mouldy cheese.

Solomon suggested the mugs had probably been topped up with piss, whilst De Flor remarked that he would rather have had his mug half empty than half filled, 'this really is the foulest liquid I've ever tasted, and I've had a few mugs of piss in my life.'

'At least we know they only have four soldiers and an officer to deal with, and I doubt if the officer is anything more than a student fresh out of college,' De Flor kept his voice low in case a soldier was guarding the hut's only door. 'I hoped we could have talked our way out trouble, I wanted to avoid violence if at all possible; try the door to make sure it's locked,' De Flor asked Solomon, who after testing the handle confirmed the door was indeed securely closed with a wooden toggle. They checked the interior of the hut for any weakness in the structure. The timber building had been hurriedly constructed, hence the flimsy way the uprights were pinned together, although there wasn't a window both men could peer through the gaps between the wooden structure and it was just possible to slide their fingers between the planks that made up the walls. With the lack of a window the walls were hastily constructed from cheap wood - no doubt pine - and probably from old, damaged dunnage timber nailed together to form an a shaky unstable storage unit.

146

De Flor kicked a chair across the room in frustration, which brought a quick response from the guard. The young sentry on guard duty wore a grim frightened face; it looked like he was trying to grow a beard to make him look older than he was, the curly blond hair on his chin failed to impress De Flor or Solomon.

'Behave or I'll stick you with my blade,' he growled at Solomon, unaware it was De Flor who had kicked the chair which lay in bits across the rotten spongy floor of the hut. The sentry left the storage unit and once again stood outside to return to his duties.

Solomon queried why they were wasting time stuck inside the hut. It would be easy to stow a couple of planks, quickly render the guard unconscious, before stealing a boat and sail out of Grand-Fort-Philippe to the open waters of the channel. Solomon continued his moaning, 'it will be dark soon. We could be well clear before they change sentries.'

De Flor could see the sense in what Solomon was saying, 'as long as we don't kill the bloody guard, just tap him on the head the send him to sleep early, otherwise the rest of them will be crawling all over the port looking for us.'

The deed was carried out like professional soldiers out on a Sunday afternoon picnic. The guard was out for the count - sleeping softly and dreaming about the village whores. Solomon thought it sensible to start a fire from the braziers, there was plenty of cotton around to ensure the fire spread, but De Flor thought it best not to endanger lives or property for if they did the whole of the royalist army would be on their trail like bloodhounds after the prey. Let's keep it simple, we render him unconscious and escape, that's all we need.

Solomon and De Flor scrambled about in the darkness of the Quayside checking for anything that might be used as a weapon or small dingy to steal. Upon finding the latter, they swiftly untied the small tender boat and headed for the canal entrance a mere hundred yards along the quay and open water when they heard voices. There didn't appear any anxiety in their talk so it looked as though the guard hadn't been woken from his dreams of lovemaking to a heavenly virgin. De Flor whispered, 'let's pull over to the far bank of the canal.' Although he hadn't noticed any bridge connecting the two banks, he didn't want to take anything for granted, 'I feel sure the opposite bank won't have any soldiers guarding it, for I cannot see any building to shelter them from the elements.'

Once the noises calmed down the two men rowed as if the devil himself was tracking them. It didn't take too long to reach open water. They heard the warning shouts a second time far behind them, but it no longer mattered as the two men were now safe from their pursuers. They were now free to tackle the last leg of their retreat to the coastline of England, and to shake hands with George Ward aboard the Falcon.

De Flor and Solomon felt giddy and lightheaded from the perpetual motion of the boat, it didn't help not knowing in which direct the boat was heading. 'Any more of this, De Flor gagged, 'and I'll pump up my breakfast,' Solomon reminded him that he hadn't eaten breakfast, 'just get on with it, once you are aboard the Falcon you will feel as right as rain.'

But in which direction was the Falcon anchored, it was too dark due to the lack of moonlight in the dense murky sky. Without the stars to assist his navigation De Flor felt totally naked, as he began to shiver, not through cold, but through fear. The night gloom of shadowing cloud kept covering the moon transferring the sphere in the sky into a mock dance. The night sky appeared forbidding and evil; this was not the type of night to go blindly across the channel.

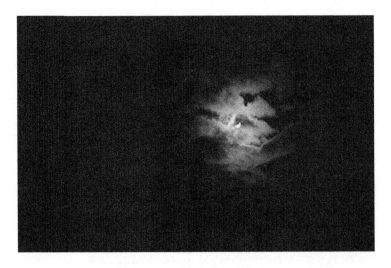

O moon, adored of old.

O Moon, adored of old, discreetly, by our sires,
from darkness above us, where, in a glittering train,
Sandaled with gold, revealed through veils of delicate rain,
the stars attend your steps and wait on your evil desires.

Based on the poem 'Flowers of evil'

Chapter Eleven

Erratic and impulsive

Once out into the open waters of the channel the sea became choppy with white horses swiftly appearing atop the waves. The tide was teasing the wind for superiority. The spray felt salty and what's more the weather was changing, it had started to drizzle. Tonight the elements were mocking De Flor, but Solomon had seldom been in the British waters, his sailing days had been limited to the Mediterranean; that is not to say the Mediterranean always had its fair share of alternating settings, from bright favourable sunny weather, the weather would change and you had to deal with the unexpected alarming volatile transformation of rage within the enclosed sea. Many a good sailor had drowned within that unpredictable and fickle seaway. You always had to respect the sea. Never take it for granted at your peril.

De Flor wasn't happy being out in the channel at this time of year and in this type of small craft. To start with the wind appeared to be light, but he knew the channel was erratic and impulsive to those who earned their living from its deep waters. De Flor was an experienced sailor, but after suffering his latest setback in their quest to reunite with the Falcon they had stupidly taken one risk too many and walked into a foolish trap. It was just as well the port of Grand-Fort-Philippe had only been secured by weak, inexperienced boys, some of them were lacking in the basic skills of life, they were so fearful of losing their virginity with the local maidens they hadn't experienced their first loving embrace or schoolboy kiss, let alone their first hug under the bedclothes. They were immature weaklings, lacking in spirit to fight a man's fight.

The weather quickly deteriorated, with the offshore waves, creating grave hazards. The wave's offshore turbulently mixed with the strong wind blowing shoreward created a monster of ground swell formulating a double surge of seemingly boiling frothy foam-covered sea. It was near impossible to remain seated or row in the small rowing boat they acquired. The troughs were particularly dangerous to navigate and steer through, one minute you felt you were down in the depths, the next exhilarated by the height of the waves pushed us up. We had to be careful not to break our flimsy rudder; otherwise we would have been left to the elements like a cork bobbing up and down. Only God knew where we were being taken. I caught a glimpse of Solomon praying in the watery bottom of the boat, 'which way is east, he shouted, but it was impossible to tell. 'Just bloody pray for the two of us this night.

Suddenly the tide changed, it had started to flood as opposed to ebb, and the change of tide coupled with the wind direction had taken the best part of the sting out of the storm. At last they were able to bail the boat out and start rowing, although God only knew where they were headed, for all they knew they could have been rowing in circles. The sea spray and the old moon had blocked their sight of land which left the English shoreline obscured. To their relief the drizzle had stopped, but the moon still failed to assist them in their quest.

With the wind strength diminished and the sea still being stubbornly unpredictable as it was in March and April, with oars in their calloused hands De Flor and Solomon made slow headway madding their way bit by bit in a northwesterly direction and eventually reached land somewhere on the South coast of England.

The Samphire Hoe beach was George's favourite anchoring location, it being protected from any northerly gales and that was where they hoped to gain knowledge of the whereabouts of the Falcon.

Samphire Hoe covered a 30-hectare site at the foot of the famous Shakespeare Cliff, situated between Dover and Folkestone. The Hoe was seldom visited in the winter and early spring time; it was only in the height of summer that the locals enjoyed picnics to help them forget their troubles and worries regarding the likelihood of another war with France. Not that there were too many locals to worry about, the site was normally devoid of onlookers except for the watermen, fishermen and custom men who travelled along the south shoreline beneath the white cliffs that confirmed to everyone they were back in England.

De Flor wondered what flag George would signal. The dark background with the white skull and crossbones was innovative that to the inexperienced onlooker they would fail to recognise or understand its meaning. Even De Flor's crew had difficulty in understanding its meaning, however, both Solomon and De Flor now understood the truth, and the significance always fitted within De Flor's scheme. If the flag failed to instill terror in the hearts of their enemies, he would, in the future, inform everyone that the skull and crossbones were something to be reckoned with representing De Molay death skull, and he crossed bones symbolised the wrath of his curse on France. The devil would reach out to obtain his curse on all those who stood by whilst the Templars were murdered in Paris.

Solomon had his head bowed under the strain of continuous rowing when he lifted his head high as he listened to De Flor's devilish curse. 'Are the English that stupid to believe in an unseen and unproven force they think might bring about harmful, painful, or unpleasant dealings?

Next you will tell me that from this day on, the thirteenth day of the month if falling on a Monday will bring forth evil and bad luck.

De Flor tried his hardest to champion the English; it's not that they are afraid; it's more a case of being browbeaten from the Church pulpit by their priests. If the priest told them that Christ will come next week, they wouldn't argue the fact, but be in readiness of his second coming.

The drizzle ceased and the day slowly turned into a cloudless bright blue over the channel. Solomon stood in the unsteady boat and shouted 'white cliffs dead ahead.'

'Do you see any ships at anchor,' De Flor asked, it was more important to site the Falcon than bloody white cliffs. White cliffs were abundant in this part of the world. 'No ships,' answered Solomon and he sat down before the light tossing of the waves forced him to fall down. Whilst he regained his composure Solomon enquired where the Roman's landed a century ago, it couldn't be here because of the mountainous white cliffs.

The Roman general Julius Caesar landed in Pegwell Bay, which is much further along the coast on the eastern side of Cent or as the British call it, Kent. If you marched from Pegwell you would need to pass through the marshy landscape of east Kent and the marshlands where the hamlets of Woodnesborough, Eastry, Eythorne, Whitfield stand. From Whitfield the distance is shortly before arriving at Dover which in turn is only a few miles further east from where we intending to land. The Roman's would have marched in double quick time and taken the enemy no more than eighteen hours in full pack.

Solomon wondered what had beaten the Roman legion's bearing in mind their invincibility. 'That's easy,' boasted De Flor, 'he wasn't defeated by the hands of the British, Caesar simply suffered from the British weather, it was too cold for him and his men.'

Solomon scratched his balding head and said, 'fancy that the might of the Roman army, led by its greatest general being beaten by the cold English weather, no wonder the Emperor Hadrian had to build a wall further north to stop his Roman soldiers from trespassing into a harsher territory. Poor soldiering if you ask me, too many nights wrapped in their cots and blankets in camp, keeping warm instead of fighting the naked warriors who never caught a cold, no wonder they got soft and retreated all the way back to Rome.

The small boat crunched on the shore of Samphire Hoe allowing the two men to steady themselves on the slippery rocks, both felt unbalanced before their natural senses took over.

'It's good to stand on English soil again,' De Flor was a happy man. Ever since the burning in Paris his sour mood had followed him step by step along the journey, but today he wore a smile.

'Not very pleasant this place called Samphire,' Solomon complained. 'Well, it's better than mainland France, where there is a likely price on our heads,' De Flor retorted, but I don't think that is true because I was reported dead back in 1305 and they can't kill me twice, and for God's sake how many Solomon's are there in the Jewish state.'

'Many,' Solomon happily answered.

'Let's get moving, which way is east, Solomon queried.

'In which direction did the sun rise this morning Jew?'

Solomon looked puzzled, or was this another riddle from his Sicilian superior?

De Flor was impatient for an answer and gave Solomon a cheeky slap about his rosy red checks.

'The sun always rises in the east and sets in the west you idiot, or am I the monkey's arse.' Luckily, De Flor was in a happy mood or he might have given Solomon another slap about his rosy red cheeks, and this time harder.

De Flor remembered an old English poem that although sung about a long time ago, he still recalled inside his head. He sat down on the rocky shoreline and receipted it to Solomon, as he had frequently receipted to Ramon many years ago when he was a fierce warrior, would he believe he had converted, not by religion but by temperament.

*****

'Then the slaughter-wolves waded - caring not for the water - the Viking army, westward across the Pante, across the bright waters, carrying their board-shields,sailing men to the shore, bearing yellow linden. There they stood ready against the ferocious one,

159

Byrhtnoth and his warriors. He ordered them to form a shield wall with their shields and for the army to hold fast against their foes. Then was the fighting near, glory in battle. The time had come when every enemy of England must fall here.'

*****

When finished, De Flor stood, faced east and called out, the tide will not be out all day, when it floods be careful of being trapped within its eddies - 'onwards Solomon, son of Solomon. How many generations of Solomon's are there?'

'Thousand's,' Solomon replied

'What if George anchored west from here,' Solomon politely asked.

'Then we will never find him,' Roger replied in disgust.

The flag

Chapter Twelve
Look and learn

Solomon had something on his mind and he couldn't hold back any longer, he had to confront De Flor with what was bothering him. 'You have noticeably changed since those early days in Le Rochelle. You appear to be more tolerant and understanding of others, the Roger I knew would have, with hesitation, stuck a blade between the shoulder blades of that young guard back in the port of Grand-Fort-Philippe and as for you turning your back on your swashbuckling days in favour of peace and tranquillity is simply not like you. Perhaps you have eaten something that disagrees with your gut!'

De Flor was annoyed and didn't like Solomon interfering or questioning his every move. 'Don't worry about me Jew; those burnings in Paris have distorted my outlook on everything. You have to remember that De

Molay was a good friend and a mentor to me, how they can sleep at night is beyond me - doing what they did to a seventy year old man - he was old enough to be their grandfather. Rest assured they will pay for their heinous crimes. I apologise if my demeanour is out of character, please be patient with me.'

Solomon considered his friends reply, and felt happy that De Flor's abruptness had been brought out into the open, however, he still felt his friend was holding back on him.

They had been walking for just under an hour, keeping one eye on the white cliffs on their left and a sharper eye on the incoming tide. They had just reached the tiny outpost of Aycliffe when Solomon shouted in excitement, 'ship ahoy.'

De Flor immediately felt his stress being released from his shoulders, he hadn't told Solomon but he was worried they had been walking in the wrong direction, but it wouldn't do to show his incompetency in front of his inferior. They hadn't been on the Falcon's decks for such a long time, and both men showed acute signs of being homesick for their beloved vessel.

A small boat was swiftly lowered into the water and immediately struck out for the shore. George was holding the tiller arm as the launch momentarily touched shore, allowing Solomon and De Flor to scramble on board, and without further ado the crew back-rowed to quickly steer the boat into deeper water before striking back to the Falcon.

There was great excitement aboard the craft as George hugged De Flor before Solomon joined in the merriments, at one stage the boat nearly capsized, but once common sense had been restored they were soon back alongside the Falcon. Everybody was clapping and singing as the two prodigal sons returned home, George especially was wearing a broad grin across his face. The crew wanted to hear of their adventures; suddenly De Flor broke down in tears before them as he recalled the De Molay's final moments. 'He did curse them as he said he would,' the second mate asked.

'Yes, but a fat load of good that did, the majority of the onlookers were held way back, they wouldn't have heard a thing. If they were there to witness men being burnt to death, they would be disappointed. At such a distance it was impossible to see much except the brightness of the fires. It was all over in less than fifteen minutes. De Molay took longer to die, 'I am sure the King ordered a long, lingering death for our Grand Master.' The men who had gathered about De Flor and Solomon openly wept, and swore oaths of vengeance against Philip and the Catholic Church before they slowly dispersed. The Templars stayed awhile they were inconsolable. The impossible had happened - they no longer had a Grand Master to guide them. They no longer had a country to fight for, they no longer held the church sacred, but they did have a flag to fight for - the skull and crossbones!

De Flor ordered all non-essential crewmembers back to their station with the exception of Solomon the Jew; he had need to converse with his officers, of which he considered Solomon one.

They squatted around De Flor in one large circle on the deck, he pointed to Solomon calling him 'the alpha' and pointed to the officer to his right stating you are now my 'omega' - 'you are my beginning and my end, as long as the sun shines bright in the heavens above as it slowly makes its journey across the sky, we are all members of a sacred crew. Your mission is to sail the Falcon north to meet up with Ramon. Hopefully he is safely anchored off Dùn Èideann with his small fleet, no doubt the locals have been concerned why they have not moved or threatened the coastline around Edinburgh. Once they cite a new ship joining them, they will have grave concerns, but we mean peace and sanctuary and the Scottish King will offer us that sanctuary.'

George is the constant worry that he was asked his skipper, 'what makes you so sure these Scots will offer us peace and sanctuary. I've heard rumours about the way they fight, they scream at their enemy as if the Satan himself is in their souls.'

'They will offer peace and sanctuary to us, don't worry your pretty head about that,' De Flor replied, 'they will offer us friendship and their women.'

George remained suspicious regarding the skipper's claims, until De Flor reminded him that the Pope hadn't especially ex-communicated any individual in Scotland, 'the bugger has ex-communicated the whole country.'

'Can he do that,' Solomon queried.

'He can, and he did,' De Flor laughed, which brought a chorus of hilarity on the decks. 'One other thing, gentlemen, he is on a sacred mission, we will spread the truth concerning the King of France and the Catholic Church and its Pope. We will shout it from the roof tops how they subjected thousands of knights to torture and death, and I will try to explain to them and you here today the true meaning of the holy cross. No doubt I will be hanged, drawn and quartered for spreading heresy, but I have faith in God and Scotland that the truth cannot kill you.

De Flor gathered his emotions and took a deep breath before continuing. 'Gaze up at our flag, that will help me explain the facts to you'. Our Lord Jesus Christ was not crucified on a cross; his final hour was spent hanging from a tau.'

'What's a tau,' he heard an officer remark?

'The Roman's didn't want to waste timber in murdering Jews, they didn't warrant that luxury.' He saw Solomon laugh at his words. 'Therefore why do we daub ourselves our mantles and shields with the sign of the cross?'

'Some of our Jewish brothers didn't warrant the tau, a single stake or tree stump was good enough for them to be nailed to.'

De Flor couldn't help but notice bewilderment on the faces of his officers and friends.

'Brothers I will tell you the origin of the cross.' De Flor had secretly requested a young cabin boy to go below and bring his heavy box from his cabin. De Flor held the box to his heart before lowering it onto the deck of the Falcon. He held the minds of his officers in the palms of his hands as he slowly lifted the lid of the ossuary. Look and learn my friends and tell me what you see?'

George being the senior officer was the first the peer into the ossuary. He had never previously seen such a sight - the bones of a long lost individual with the last relics placed neatly in the form of - the skull and crossbones.' George turned to De Flor and asked, 'what does it signify captain?'

De Flor asked his first officer to look again and take notice of what he was seeing.

George sat in amazement until he it suddenly dawned on him what his Captain was asking of him - 'the crossbones' with a skull atop,' he whispered.

'Preciously, the skull and crossbones, these are not symbols of death and destruction, although many will consider them to be such. They are the sign of resurrection, just like our Lord was resurrected.' With his lecture ended De Flor looked worn out as he sat back down again with his close friends.

The deck remained silent as everyone was trying to accept and take in what had just been put before them, some readily accepted De Flor's conclusions, others sat in quiet bewilderment, only a few thought about arguing with De Flor, but as they were unable to offer any constructive alternatives, they like the rest sat in silence.

With the ossuary safely back in his protective hands De Flor stood, offered his apologies, saying he needed to sleep and disappeared through the small door the led to his cabin.

The crew slowly dispersed mumbling to each other or themselves, they had a lot to think about, some would find it hard to sleep tonight, whilst others like George Ward had accepted everything that was said and until it was his time to be on watch he would sleep soundly.

The crossed bones?

The Cross of St. Andrew of Scotland

Chapter thirteen

Living in constant fear at Lindisfarne

Take us on a nor-easterly course until we are clear Dover, and then bring us up on a straight northerly course to clear Kent's easterly point at the village of Broadstow. Hold us off shore Mister Ward, let's not accidentally ground ourselves upon any of the nasty sand banks that have wrecked many a vessel along Kent's coastline.

'They call it Broadstairs now captain, don't the why, the English are a fickle lot,' Ward smiled as he explained the indecisiveness of his foe across the channel. 'It gets worse skipper, there is no longer a village called Remisgat, after the old lady of the manor Christina de Remmesgate, it seems she died and no one took on the right to call themselves Remmesgate so they simply forgot her and they now call he dung heap Ramisgate or Raunsgate, but young Richard, the sail makers apprentice tells me the name Ramsgate seems to have borne favour with the locals.'

De Flor thought long and hard about his reply and eventually called out, 'no wonder the damn English always get lost in Europe.'

Solomon looked embarrassed as he stood next to his Captain, he knew some offence would soon be directed in his direction, and so it did - 'you lot got lost in the desert for forty years Solomon. Forty bloody years, damn useless navigators if you ask me,'

De Flor went below to his day cabin muttering away to himself as he purposely made as much noise as possible to let his fellow officers aware of his departure. De Flor found the town's name fascinating, he thought the origins of the name was easy, it comes from the late Anglo-Saxon words for raven, meaning hræfn or hemmes, and the word gate meaning geat, which had reference to a gap in the cliffs. If his crew studied history as much as killing they would be aware of where they were headed.

The Falcon slowly passed the East Anglian coast on its port side, eventually sailing past the great watery expanse of the wash, where King John lost his crown. The King became ill and decided to go back. While he took the long route through Wisbech, he sent his luggage, including his crown jewels, along the coastal road and across the mouth of the Wellstream where the water was not deep. This route was only safe when the tide was low. The horse-drawn wagons moved too slowly for the incoming tide, and many were lost. The whole area at the time was an extensive wetland known as The Fens, which was later drained. It is close to sea level. Somewhere in that mucky sand laid undisturbed a vast fortune waiting to be found, many had, and many had failed. The King's ransom will only show itself to the world on judgement day, but De Flor had no idea what God Almighty needed with gold.

The Falcon anchored off Skegness, the easterly point of Lincolnshire, to take on fresh water. While he waited for the boats to return with fresh water and provisions, De Flor pondered over the originality of such a flea bitten fishing village as Skeggness. He knew the town and deep, long routes as William the Bastard recorded the shit hole village within stupid Doomsday book. Skegg or Skeggi's headland had been spoken about for ages. De Flor being well versed in Danish culture knew a skegg simply meant beard, so no doubt whoever the first settlers in the town were ruled over by a shaggy bearded Viking. If there was anything additional to be known about the place and the man it would have more than likely been washed miles away by the unforgiving and thieving sea. If De Flor passed this way ten years from now he wouldn't recognise the landscape - houses and taverns built of timber on sand wouldn't stand a chance against the ever advancing currents of the German Ocean.

The Falcon was well stocked with one hundred water barrels, fresh vegetables, some scrawny chickens, and a dozen piglets, more than enough to get us to Edinburgh.

At the mouth of the Humber off the Spurn, De Flore suggested we relaxed to practice the art of fishing, not as a sporting pastime, but the Captain knew a change in our dietary intake would prove beneficial for our well being. The fish that day seemed to commit suicide by jumping onto our hooks is if they bait was fit for a king.

It had taken over a week to sail around the coast of Kent until we anchored off the Spurn; to date, no one had challenged our reason for sailing up the coast of England, until now.

Whilst the men enjoyed fishing and singing songs that reminded them of home, where ever home might be, a small boat rowed out to come alongside our starboard side.

De Flor looked down with distrust, 'fucking customs boat, no doubt they want to know where we are going and details of our cargo, the in's and out's of a ducks arsehole.'

'Ahoy there Falcon, permission to come aboard,' De Flor recommended to leave the talking to him alone. 'They are bloody leeches, but I suppose they are just doing their job.'

Two men boarded using the Jacob ladder we let flow down to their custom boat. After the usual pleasantries the custom's officer in charge introduced himself as Adolphus Dobner, an Austrian who had settled within the town and married a local woman. Adolphus looked well dressed and well mannered, but he represented officialdom and De Flor hated officialdom.

'Your last port of call Captain?' De Flor quickly stated Tangiers.

'Your destination, Captain?' 'Edinburgh we have a cargo of salmon to unload in Gibraltar.'

'How many persons do you have aboard,' De Flor had to check that for he didn't know if any had jumped ship. I'll check that with my sailing Master, but I know we saved two you Negro girls from certain death in the Atlantic, not far from the port of Tangiers.

George Ward came to stand alongside Adolphus and informed the customs officer of their current numbers.

'Everything seems to be in order Captain, but pray tell me the origins of the flag you fly.'

De Flor had to think quick, 'as my crew originates from various countries, we thought it a reasonable request from them to fly a flag recognised for our faith in a one God.'

'A most sincere and heartfelt sentiment Captain, I wish you good sailing and a safe arrival in Edinburgh. You have been at sea for so long that I doubt if you have heard of the atrocities in your homeland?'

De Flor answered that his homeland was in Germany, and he was unaware of recent events at home.

Adolphus apologised, wrongly think he was from France. 'A very sad state of affairs in France, it seems their King had executed his Knights, or to be correct his Knights Templar, he has slain every last one of them.'

'Not every last one of them,' De Flor thought to himself, 'if I am not mistaken, I still breathe the good air of England.'

Adolphus climbed down the Jacobs ladder and bid them farewell, 'safe journey,' he heard as the boat came clear from the Falcon. News travels fast between France and England

George came back to stand beside De Flor, 'it seems King Philip is under the impression he has killed of the Templars, might be best to remain in Scotland once our journey has been completed, although I still don't understand why Scotland should attract you as it does.'

'George, order the crew to fill the baskets with the fish and salt them well, we set sail for Scotland in fifteen minutes, open one water barrel and let the men quench their thirst.

The sails were now full of wind and our passage was going well. We waved to the women who stood on the docksides of Whitby, Hartlepool and the old lighthouse warning off ships from the sand and rocks of the entrance to the Tyne. Eventually the tranquil island of Lindisfarne came into view. How many times had the Danes thrashed and slaughtered the islanders, but as soon as the Danes left with their ill-gotten treasure the monks returned. You had to admire their persistence and determination, but every year the Danes came back and after they left the monks returned, such a cruel cycle of life they lived, knowing that death would annually revisit their island. Their only hope seemed to rest in God accepting the Norse hordes as members of his ever extending congregation.

Solomon was on duty as they passed Lindisfarne, 'your God certainly moves in mysterious ways.'

I have little doubt both our God's move in mysterious ways, but it is not up to us to doubt or question him.' With that final remark De Flor was back in his day cabin, locking the door behind him.

Solomon thought to himself, 'the Captain either seeks solitude or he has so many dark shadows to overcome.'

The ruins at Lindisfarne

Chapter Fourteen

Lindisfarne
The Holiest of Islands

'I should like to go ashore to these Lindisfarne Islands,' after he unlocked his day cabin to shade his eyes from the sun's brightness.

They tell me if you shut your eyes tight and think mesmerize the past you can hear and fill your heart and soul with the visualization of the good and bad things that has occurred within its history.'

Both George and Solomon wanted to join their Captain by rowing across one hundred yards of water to gain access to the main island.

With the collapse of the countless Northumbrian kingdoms the monks of Lindisfarne fled the island in 875 taking with them the holy relic bones of St. Cuthbert's which they reburied with as much pomp and ceremony beneath the nave of Durham cathedral. The monks of Lindisfarne had the foresight to lay a fine foundation stone in readiness for a castle, which when sufficient funds became available to build the castle, work would commence soon to offer added protection atop the hillside alongside the old priory.

Access to the island was only possible at low water, when it was safe to walk across the causeway connecting the mainland to the island, or as in our case a small boat would convey us three safely ashore. However, if you attempted to gain entry onto Lindisfarne when the stone causeway was under the sea and invisible to the naked eye your journey will forever remain inside your buried memories. De Flor followed in the very footsteps that our ancient monks, who built their priory here nearly 1,400 years ago. He explored the wild and weather worn coastal beauty of Holy Island. He stood transfixed awhile to visualise the fascinating culture of the very men who were doomed to the annual slaughter in the hope that one day the grisly Viking raiders would accept the way of the one God of Christianity and his prophet St Cuthbert in particular, especially his beautiful manuscript outlining the Lindisfarne Gospels.

As the tide swirled about the muddy foundations of the castle and priory the solitude of the monks was guaranteed. The three visitors heard music playing from within the bowls of the chapel, however, they were soon corrected as no musical instrument had ever been stored on the island. The beautiful soulful sounds were brought together by delightful harmonies relating to the chants of the days long before the axe and superseded the word of God, but the inhabitants had never forgotten they always remembered.

De Flor kept his eyes tight shut; he didn't want anything to get in the way of the heavenly music orchestrated by the monks. Holy Island, as the locals preferred to call it, was an important centre of Celtic Christianity under Saints Aidan, Cuthbert, Eadfrith and Eadberht of Lindisfarne. After the Viking's invaded, followed by the foul Norman conquest of England, the priory had been reestablished in the design of the old. The island of Lindisfarne is located along the northeast coast of England, close to the border with Scotland. Lindisfarne is known as the big island or Holy Island with a group twelve or lesser known uninhabited islands offering it scant protection from the Norse raiders.

Cuthbert died on 20 March 687 and was buried in a stone coffin inside the main church on Lindisfarne. Eleven years later the monks opened his tomb. To their delight they discovered that Cuthbert's body had not decayed, but was 'incorrupt,' a sure sign, they argued, of his purity and saintliness. His remains were elevated to a coffin-shrine at ground level, and this marked the beginnings of the cult of St Cuthbert, which was to alter the course of Lindisfarne's history.

Miracles were soon reported at St Cuthbert's shrine and Lindisfarne was quickly established as the major pilgrimage centre in Northumbria. As a result, the monastery grew in power and wealth, attracting grants of land from kings and nobles as well as gifts of money and precious objects

All this was before De Flor time as he now stood astride the ruined priory roof; he felt himself going into a trance like daze which eventually took over his spiritual body. He heard screams and cries, murders and burnings, swords scraping along the wall and cutting into bone. He felt a connection with the island, a connection that failed to leave him until his dying day. When he reopened his eyes he felt his body relax and completely overcome; a feeling of being cleansed by an overwhelming spirit of God. The experience was totally alien from his youth when he spent days practicing his sword arm, enabling him to kill without mercy. He shuddered at the thought. He repeated to him, but was unable to understand the words; he had never muttered them before, but they came from his lips loud and clear, startling George and Solomon -

'The cult of St Cuthbert consolidated the monastery's reputation as the principle centre for

Christian learning. The result of which was produced in six hundred years ago of a masterpiece known as the earliest medieval art known as the 'Lindisfarne Gospels.' De Flor rolled his eyes whereby only the white faced forward. Solomon and George were deeply afraid thinking that their Captain was suffering from epilepsy.

He spoke in a strange tongue, De Flor noticed the strangeness within his voice and in his thinking he suspected God was walking through him as he predicted the following -

'Jerusalem will never fall into Christian hands again.'

'The power of the Muslim will retain not diminish over the Dome of The Rock for many centuries - until God in his wisdom will bring forth his thunder and brightness and an overpowering eruption of death. Man will yet again forsake the wisdom of The Almighty.'

'The Jews will have to illuminate their actions the One God, for their actions. Jerusalem will be erased from the surface of the earth, for I have seen this, and hear me - it will come to fruition once we touch the third millennium, unless the box can be positioned atop the invisible flowered cable.'

One and the same.
The Dome of the Rock or
The Temple Mount in Jerusalem.
The holiest place for Jews, Muslims and Christians.

Chapter Fifthteen

Newhaven

Once back aboard the Falcon we expressed our amazement at what we had witnessed and the wonderment at what our eyes beheld on Lindisfarne. De Flor explained the island was truly the holiest and blessed place on earth, even Solomon agreed with his Captain's sentiments. The Christian's within the crew requested the Falcon remained at anchor to enable them to visit the island and pray in the priory, even the Jews and the followers of Islam wanted to go ashore, just for the incredible views, and to steady their legs on solid ground.

De Flor was happy to respond positively to their request and the tender boat and our small jolly boat were lowered in unison to allow our international crew plenty of time to gaze upon the beauty of Lindisfarne. We sail on the top of the tide, by my calculations that will be six of the clock this evening.

At six o'clock the crew was all at their posts, ready to haul up the anchor and standing to on the rigging for unfurling the sails. De Flor was delighted with the way the crew would follow him no matter where or when he sailed. It was through no fault of their own that they were all marked men, arrest warrants were circulating throughout France for those who followed the outlawed Templar known at Roger de Flor. Every member of the crew knew their families would be under suspicion and watched, just in case they any of them tried to return to France. However, De Flor told them that in due time he would endeavour to send messengers to France telling them their men folk were safe and waiting for them in Scotland should they so desire.

The Falcon sailed serenely on a northerly course, sailing past the Tweed, the last English harbour, on their port side. They followed the coastline as close as possible. They clearly saw the locals waving and cheering them as they passed, they were enthusiastically welcomed them north of the border as though they were the saviours come to join in their deadly quest against the dreaded English.

At Dunbar De Flor gave orders to navigate to port in readiness for entering the Leith River. There was a large natural harbour ahead, we will moor there, De Flor smiled as he pointed to his chart.

The location that he pointed at was Newhaven, two miles north of Edinburgh.

Solomon shut his eyes and pinched his nose, making sure he couldn't take in the stench of gutted fish - not another fishing village. As the Falcon touched alongside the quay, George was surprised by the way the locals seemed to turn out to assist in the moorings; in no time at all three head ropes, two stern ropes and spring ropes fore and aft were heaved up tight. The sails were made fast on their respective cross beams as the sailors tried to impress the local females who waved back at the bravery of the men, not that the sailors were brave, they were just showing off.

The local harbour master and other town dignitaries made their way up the gangplank to be welcomed personally by the smiling Captain Roger De Flor.

'Welcome, welcome,' the harbour master kept repeating himself, 'welcome to Scotland. We have been tracking your progress since you passed the Tweed. I sincerely hope you have not been tormented by any English vessels.' The mayor of Newhaven pointed skywards, as his eyes settled on the black and white flag fluttering on our mainmast. 'Pray tell me Captain, what country's flag do you fly?'

De Flor smiled back, informing the mayor and the harbour master that he flew the flag of Jesus Christ; we have all suffered under the teachings of the Catholic Church, especially in their continuous attempts of expunging us from the face of the world. We are mainly former Templars, as for the rest of my crew, they are loyal to me and I to them, no matter what God they fight for. Their God is my God, we understand each other's values and most importantly, we share a righteous God content in His ethics of peace and tranquility, my crew is in total harmony with each other - no Captain can ask for more.'

'Please forgive my rudeness Mister Mayor I was hoping my compatriots would be berthed somewhere close by. We left France some time ago, my journey took me to Malta and the North African coast before arriving in Scotland, whereas they sailed directly to Leith, or as you prefer to call it the Moray Firth of Forth.'

The mayor looked stunned as he tried to explain that a particularly nasty pestilence had left its mark on Newhaven three years ago. The local doctors had tried their best to contain the source of the sickness and decided it would be safer for the local residents if the ships moored within the harbour should depart and anchor offshore. Three years ago we had more than nine vessels within our harbour; they all sailed away to anchorages further downstream, most likely Musselburg, a small village five miles due east from here. Once the epidemic had safely passed your friends might be moored within its natural harbour. If your friends were in Musselburg harbour I doubt if you would have seen them at low tide.

'Don't worry,' the harbour master informed De Flor, ' I will send riders along the coast to see if your friends are still there, I should have news within a couple of hours.

De Flor thanked the mayor and the harbour master for their assistance, all he could do was sit and wait, but waiting was not one of De Flor's attributes.

While the mayor and harbour waited patiently for their messengers to return, they explained to De Flor that the sickness blew through town on am evil wind from the east, there was nothing they could do to contain the spread of sickness. Since the time of ancient Egypt, smallpox has proven to be one of the most devastating diseases ever known to humankind. Widespread smallpox epidemics and huge death tolls fill the pages of our parish burial books. There were so many townsfolk killed by the disease, which became known as the smallpox, that the churchyards were full to capacity, we eventually had to burn the bodies as the corpses retained to ability to kill. By the time the plague left well over two hundred and fifty-three local inhabitants had succumbed, including my wife and three children.

The mayor's conversation was cut short by the return of the first rider. He informs me that over half of your men were struck down by the pox; the survivors are safely aboard your ships moored in Musselburg harbour. The Bruce's private physician and his staff have been looking after them. Those who died were buried far out to sea to enable the living to do just that - live! 'I'll tell you one thing though, every last one of those ships fly an identical flag to you. I wonder how that could be!'

The mayor had genuine signs of loss about his eyes as he told De For - 'I am sorry for your loss.'

De Flor eyes meet with the mayors as he replied, - and I for yours.'

Eventually De Flor regained his voice once again, 'is there room enough in Musselburg for one more ship Mister Mayor? I have to ascertain how many of my men died; I am most anxious to trace a man, his name was Ramon Muntaner, a Catalan, he was my chronicler.

The Mayor appeared shocked, 'you have not heard Captain.'

'Heard what; I have not heard very much since we parted company in La Rochelle eight years ago.'

'Well then I will speak slowly so that you can collate every scrap of news and evidence; Mister Ramon is not at Musselburg, he left with the Bruce's brother in Ireland last year with over 200 men. The Bruce campaign was a three-year military campaign in Ireland by Edward Bruce, brother of the Scottish king Robert the Bruce. It lasted from his landing at Larne in 1315 It skirmish was part of the First War of Scottish Independence that brought conflict with the Irish and the Anglo-Normans. I fear the fighting in Ireland is not going well.

Bannockburn had been considered as our greatest triumph, however, your Templar cavalry turned the tide of battle in the Bruce's favour, otherwise I fear if a single Scottish soldier would have survived. The King told everybody that the battle was won by the Scottish Claymore, but we all knew the Templar cavalry crushed Edward's infantry. You Templars certainly know how to fight. The Scottish army was divided into three divisions of schiltrons commanded by the Bruce, his brother Edward Bruce, and his nephew, the Earl of Moray. After Robert Bruce killed Sir Henry de Bohun on the first day of the battle, the English were forced to withdraw for the night. Sir Alexander Seton, a Scottish noble serving in Edward's army, defected to the Scottish side and informed them of the English camp's position and low morale. Robert Bruce decided to launch a full-scale attack on the English forces and to use his schiltrons again as offensive units, a strategy his predecessor William Wallace had not used. The English army was defeated in a pitched battle which resulted in the deaths of several prominent commanders, including the Earl of Gloucester and Sir Robert Clifford, and captured many others.

'About the time of departure from La Rochelle, William Wallace was captured in Glasgow and conveyed to London to stand trial. Unwilling to compromise, William Wallace kept refusing to submit to English rule, and Edward's men eventually caught up with him on the August 5th 1305, He was taken to London and condemned as a traitor to the Crown. At Smithfield's he was hanged, disembowelled, beheaded and quartered. The Scottish nation was infuriated as they had no grave marker to pray for an imminent victory over our old enemy. With Wallace dead our nation soon found out how deep rock bottom was, but we turned about with the help of your fellow Templars and grave the English King a rare bloody nose.'

With Wallace gone, the Bruce has found a new lease of life; he embraces victories, as long as he takes all of the credit. We have heard that some English soldiers run away as soon as they witnessed Templars on the battlefield, but we have constantly denied this claim as lies. We wouldn't want the French King to think he had not slain every Templar on earth.

I suppose you know that King Dinis I of Portugal created an of the Order of Christ in 1317 for those knights who survived their mass slaughter in France.

In Germany the order flourished as The Order of Brothers of the German House of Saint Mary in Jerusalem, commonly the Teutonic Order is a Catholic religious order founded as a military order in about 1190 in Acre, within the Kingdom of Jerusalem. The Teutonic Order was formed to aid Christians on their pilgrimages to the Holy Land and to establish hospitals.

The Mayor carried on his conversation with De Flor, as he spoke about the rise to fame of Switzerland. The main income of Switzerland was in former times farming, it was a poor country, ripe for a takeover.

In 1315, Duke Leopold of Habsburg attacked several hundred men with his force of 2,000 knights and 9,000 foot soldiers, he was expecting next to nothing in the way of resistance. He was in for a surprise, as the Swiss possessed a new weapon, the *'Halberd.'* The weapon was similar in description to a lance which was mounted on a long pole, capable of bringing down horses. Leopold lost almost 2,000 warriors that day, and was forced to retreat. It seems highly probable that a primitive farming country must, of receiving outside assistance, enabling them to protect their lands from outside their borders.

The only feasible answer to make sense was that some Templar Knights escaped from France, and crossed the border into Switzerland where they were granted sanctuary. Their military expertise and Templar treasure bought their way into this new country.

The Templar's were Europe's bankers between the 11-14th century. That crown is now worn by the largest banking and financial institutions of Europe. Rags to riches only happen in fairy stories

'With regards to Rosslyn, I understand you wish to visit the estate, but surely you must be aware there is nothing of note to see except a ruined priory. The Earl intended to build a chapel close by, but at present, possibly through lack of funds nothing exists. You are about one hundred years too early my friend.'

Chapter Sixteen

The gift

De Flor was happy that his old friend Ramon was alive and well and doing things he enjoyed doing best - killing. The Falcon and its crew would wait at Musselburg until he returned, and then he thought, there would be some heavy heads around for many a day. These Scottish were overly keen on drink wine or strong, they preferred to drink small measures of a potent liquid called whisky. Neither De Flor, George nor Solomon had ever tasted the evil brew, for that is what the local fishermen called it, - the evil brew.

The Falcon's crew went to work repairing the sails, masts and below waterline planking. All the old water barrels were drained dry, the water looked green and slimy as it gurgled out from the large tap hole, the same was true about the food still being stores inside cupboards, they may have been lashed down to prevent them from spilling their contents into the watery bilge but the lashings had no control over the rats and mice, with the amount of shit stinking inside the bottom of the cupboards the small team of cooks could believe the beetles and vermin that must be lurking within the shadows. The only produce that was last of the chickens and a few skinny piglets less than a month old, we were now safe to restore our larders to overflowing.

The harbour master, mayor and De Flor became good friends, enjoyed each other's company whilst playing checkers or cards, but De Flor failed to like the evil brew and didn't understand why his two friends couldn't get enough of the stuff. 'It tastes like cows piss,' De Flor spoke the words aloud to make sure his friends understood, but the weather in Scotland was too cold to grow the grape vines that produced a good wine. The ale was passable it is slightly better than cows piss, he always looked out of the tavern window to check where they stored the evil whisky brew.

The summer months were not too bad, but God helps everyone in Scotland once the snow sets in. The land was rugged and demanding, the sheep and hairy cattle seemed to freely roam without fences to ensure their wanderings wasn't too far reaching.

One evening, late summer the mayor announced that Sinclair would be returning back south from the outer islands, he would lodge at his property at Rosslyn.

De Flor was much pleased by the news; he had important discussions to impart with the Earl. The mayor told him he would make the necessary arrangements, but he didn't think the Earl would be at home for another two weeks.

'That's not a problem,' De Flor laughed, 'it gives me enough time to empty your pockets of coins.'

Fifteen days later William Sinclair made his grand entrance, he was a happy man, full of energy and good humour, and he explained to De Flor that Rosslyn Chapel would be found on a small hill above Roslin Glen as a Catholic collegiate church, with between four and six ordained canons and two boy choristers. The chapel was promised to be founded by William Sinclair, 1st Earl of Caithness of the Scoto-Norman Sinclair family.

'Sinclair hoped to Sinclair found the college to celebrate the Divine Office throughout the day and night, and also to celebrate Masses for all the faithful departed, including the deceased members of the Sinclair family. During this period, the rich heritage of plainsong, a single melodic line or polyphony, a vocal harmony would be used to enrich the singing of the liturgy. Sinclair provided an endowment to pay for the support of the priests and choristers in perpetuity. The priests also had parochial responsibilities.

'Why not commence your building work now, I don't mean any offence but I do not understand your delay, unless it is to do with money.' De Flor queried.

'Such a noble cause would bring peace and prosperity to the local workforce, I assume you have sufficient masons, carpenters and all else you require?'

'You are correct Roger,' he replied, 'but money doesn't always give you the best masons and best carpenters, for my chapel I want the best labour force and materials money can buy.'

'I ask this because I have brought with me a special gift I was hoping you could deposit within the bowls of your chapel.'

William Sinclair looked surprised, 'why would you trust me with a gift, we have not long met.'

'Trust, I agree is extremely important and your people have trusted me and my fellow knights, I have much love for your people. As you know some of my men are with Edward Bruce in Ireland.'

'Ah, Edward, the King's brother, brought home in a wooden box, he lies dead in the centre of Edinburgh Cathedral.'

De Flor had expected this; all he could offer was his sincere apologies.

'I hope I am not being overly rude by asking what your gift is,' Sinclair seemed to have a distinct air of nonchalance.

'You are sitting on it,' De Flor laughed. 'It is an ossuary box I saved from being damaged when Saladin retook the city. It might have some kind of significance, I cannot tell, but it certainly looks old.'

'Some shopkeepers in Jerusalem make things look older than they are,' Sinclair still didn't look excited.

'There is an inscription on the side, but as I am unable to translate the scratching, hum, I was hoping you might help.'

Sinclair studied the scratchings for some time, his eyes failed to move away from the strange wording. 'If this is what I think it is you may have brought to Scotland something of great importance. I will need to get a second or even a third opinion from some knowledgeable men who might be able to verify this item. Call on me tonight about eight, if it is what I suspect, we will enjoy a culinary feast and drink our fill of whisky.'

Sinclair returned to the Falcon just after eight o'clock, being late summer the sun still shone in the western sky. Sinclair was with a small crowd, mainly clergy, but there was one with them that surprised De Flor.

'Good evening Mister De Flor,' Sinclair burst into laughter, it looked like he had downed too much evil brew before returning to Musselburg. 'May I introduce to you, the Arch-Bishop of Scotland, together with his most learned church archivists?'

De Flor shook hands with everyone, but the last guest had kept to the rear of the congregation, which made De Flor uncomfortable until he was finally introduced.

'May I introduce to you Robert the Bruce, King of Scotland,' as the two men clasped hands there was an instant camaraderie between the two men.

'Lord King,' De Flor knelt before the Bruce. Not knowing what else to say, De Flor gave a broad smile, he had never been happier in his entire life, he held tightly on to the King's hand, before slowly recognising the King's hand was turning blue. The Bruce reminded De Flor of Jacque de Molay, not so much in looks, but his character and attitude; he was the mentor and friend he had so cruelly lost.

Sinclair quickly came to the rescue of the Bruce. 'That ossuary you allowed me to take to Edinburgh, do you know what it stands for?' De Flor was now speechless, he was in the presence of a King, not a misguided French King, who only thought about gold and taxation, the Bruce was a fair natured and effortless Kingly.

I will write down the words for you,

ישו של אחיו ,ומרים יוסף בן יעקב.

Please forgive me; I still cannot understand the words, even though you have cleaned the stone surround.

Translated it says, -

'James, son of Joseph and Mary, brother of Jesus.'

De Flor sank to his knees, no sound came from his lips, he was in a state of shock, and unable to move or stand he was helped to his feet by the King of Scotland, the Bruce.

Once De Flor was back on his feet, his whole body started to shake, his nerves began to play games with him.

Three months after Solomon, George Ward and our Captain, Roger De Flor arrived in Musselburg, Ramon Muntaner returned from Ireland. He looked much thinner than usual, but his spirits rose at the sight of his friends. 'Ireland is no place for us sun lovers,' he joked. De Flor correctly assumed that Ireland was not on Ramon's favourite place to visit list.

George and De Flor wandered off by themselves, probably to discuss the ossuary, or other secretive location that Ramon and Solomon weren't privy too, which allowed Solomon time to talk about De Flor.

'I am not sure if I should mention this,' Solomon started his story, 'but ever since the Adriana pole our Captain has without a doubt changed, he regularly informs me that he wishes to lay down his sword forever in the pursuit of peace and understanding. When we were captured at the fishing port at Grand-Fort-Philippe Roger found it difficult to kill the guard to make our escape, he just wanted to smack him about the head to render him unconscious before we stole a boat to row across the channel. De Flor has greatly changed.'

'Well, he certainly looks and talks as he always has done.' George answered, 'I cannot propose any way he could have changed. Unless?

'Unless what,' Solomon was about to continue with his train of thought.

'De Flor had been always paranoid; he often surrounded himself with body-doubles in case there was an attempt on his life. At Adrianople there was a supposed attempt on his life. What if the assassin murdered his body-double leaving De Flor clear to slip away unseen?'

An interesting scenario, but a bit far fetched for my liking,' George quickly replied.

'We only have De Flor's explanation, perhaps it suited his desires to disappear until after the executions took place. I would have thought our Captain would be high up on the King Philip's list of people to get rid of!'

'Maybe,' George rubbed his head as he left, leaving Solomon to contemplate his mysteries.

Chapter Seventeen

The Chronicler

The summer of 1335 was extremely hot in the Mediterranean as I settled in my favourite chair on the veranda overlooking my island home in central Ibiza. The small town of Elvissa had always been good to me, giving me plenty of time and more importantly solitude to continue my life's work; all I needed was Francesca, my cleaner and cook to bring me supplies and the occasional half hour to catch up with the local gossip. My needs were very simple and exceptionally basic - food, drink, paper, ink, quills and plenty of blank sheets of paper. I had known Francesca since before the wars, she was my third cousin - or something like that; all I knew was that Francesca listened to gossip, but never spread it. I lived my life at my own gentle pace, at the age of seventy nobody could blame me - I looked old and frail. I suppose nobody imagined the adventurous, colourful and exciting life that I always took for granted and normality. Over the past fifty years during those heady days I always told Roger that the pen was mightier than the sword, but Roger failed to understand my reasoning. In those days he was at his happiest slashing away with his heavy two-handed sword, causing panic and chaos within the enemy ranks. The long broadsword was Roger's instrument of torture; he always told me better to slash than pierce a victim.

A faint smile came to my lips as I recalled the sight of Roger De Flor in full flow, he was a ferocious man, and just looking at him in action would always give him a major advantage over any opponent. It took brawn and strength to use the broadsword, unlike the fancy curved swords carried by his Islamic counterparts.

I dipped my quill into the dark ink and started to write, my quill hovered above the blank page, but I quickly laid it down again, I needed more time to formulate the words before I committed the words onto paper - once written I could never take my story back. I thought about Solomon and George; they were both much closer to Roger than me. They were both loyal friends, never giving me any opportunity to doubt their abilities as sailors or warriors, but I never really knew either of them as well as Roger. I picked up my quill again and dipped it within the ink, this time I managed to put some words on paper. I felt much saddened not to have known Solomon or George; both were loyal in the battle and good men whilst covering your back. Roger had once told me that Solomon was a member of the secretive Sicarii sect, but I had his doubts. The Sicarii were notorious in their love for slaughtering Romans, their sect being named from the small, lethal dagger they carried, and their motto of *'death before dishonour'* conjured up the thought they were fighting the demons from hell. I told Solomon he couldn't possibly be of the Sicarii sect - I couldn't accept that possibility, although he fought harder than any other on the battlefield at Bannockburn before being overpowered by four of five English infantry. They buried him in a shallow grave in the Jewish tradition; I didn't speak much Hebrew, but thought, a prayer in his native language was appropriate. I closed my eyes and looked towards the heavens and softly spoke before they covered his battered body into the dark, shadowy enclosure of a distant far from home battlefield - *Earth you are, and to earth you will return.'*

My thoughts turned to George, the English sailor, who like many of his race seemed to have water to have flowing through his veins. All Roger had to do was inform his sailing master where he wanted to go, and George Ward would get him there. Sadly, his knowledge of all other worldly traits was beyond George. He did, however, bring us news that our friends who sailed to other destinations after leaving La Rochelle.

George confirmed that a settlement had been established in the America's and another had spread itself about the islands about the Indian Ocean. However, much to the annoyance of the French king Portugal had gladly opened its arms to any Knights Templar who knocked on their door.

Prior to George sailing further north into the coastal wasteland of snow and the floating sea ice the local tribes referred to as Canada. George was an adventurer and was always keen to know what colour the grass was over the next hill. I never knew if George, the English explorer, ever reached his goal, but I knew he was at his happiest finding new lands that no living soul had ever seen before.

I sat back in my chair and spoke gently to myself, for no other person was within the house, 'George, I miss your blind goodness George, for you above all I truly miss only Roger could be a better friend.'

As God is my witness throughout my trials and tribulations these past years without my dear friend Roger De Flor I have great urgency to be put down in writing, before the truth falls into Turkish hands, for they will surely rewrite the truth, and when the truth is rewritten only lies fester. The Byzantine Empire was the target for adventurers from many nations. At the foremost of these was the Almogaver army led by friend

Roger De Flor, the army was composed of mercenaries hardened in the war between the Catalan and Angevin dynasties both had thoughts for domination of the largest island within the Mediterranean Sea - Sicily. The Catalan presence in Constantinople aroused suspicion among the Greek nobility, who everyone thought assassinated Roger De Flor, and tried to exterminate every last one of his men. I never honestly knew if Roger survived the slaughter or if his body-double deception worked. The devastating reaction of those who escaped the slaughter led to the Catalan's controlling vast swathes of the Empire, including Athens.

I was one of the agitators of the expedition, along with George Ward, Solomon the Sicarii and of course Roger De Flor, or whatever his alias, each had vital roles to play.

I left Scotland for my native Spain soon after the Bruce's victory at Bannockburn; as a chronicler in support of the truth, I could no listen to the English false propaganda machine that churned out lie after lie and continuously supported a distortion of the truth.

I had visited the Bruce two days prior to my departure, requesting his permission to return to Spain, I told him the Scottish climate didn't agree with my health. At the time the English King was spreading false rumours regarding the Bruce's health with regards to

Robert's torment from his suffering from leprosy. The English continued with their outlandish slanderous lies in their attempt to demoralise the Scots; another English smear suggested the Bruce had foreign mercenaries within their ranks when Edward's army were sent packing from the battlefield at Bannockburn. This of course was true.

The Bruce knew that the alliance he had cemented with Roger De Flor's small company of Templars had made a significant contribution to the outcome of the battle; it was simply a case of battle hardened and well trained fighting men battling against conscripted irregulars. In De Flor's mind, he knew he had tipped the scales in favour of the Bruce, but this had to be kept covert; if it became known that the Bruce could only win battles for Scottish Independence by incorporating French mercenaries into his army then the reality of Independence might be forever lost.

Gossip spreads like wildfire, claims and counterclaims circulated both sides of the border. Myths were used to show that Robert the Bruce was a weak ruler who couldn't win his own battles, in my view the Bruce was an inspirational military leader, but I could only impart that truth in my native Spain; in Scotland, I was only seen as a foreign collaborator.

I had to keep moving, my life as a former Templar and chronicler of Templar truths were constantly in danger from agents of the French King, especially after the King suffered a cerebral stroke during a hunt at Pont-Sainte-Maxence, within the Forest of Halatte. Philip died a few weeks later, on Thursday the twenty-ninth day of November 1314, at Fontainebleau, close to where he was born.

After his election as Pope in 1313, Clement V ushered in an era of French papal corruption; his death on Saturday the twentieth day of April 1314 caused unrest with the French people, however, within a year, as prophesied by Jacque De Molay, both his accusers were dead.

According to one account, while his body was lying in state, a thunderstorm arose during the night and lightning struck the church where his body lay, setting it on fire. The fire was so intense that by the time it was extinguished, the Pope's body had been all but destroyed. What was left of the Templar movement thought this poetic justice for our Grand Master who was consumed by fire the previous year. The corrupt pope was buried at the collegiate church in Uzeste, as laid down in his will, close to his birthplace in Villandraut.

The French people saw these two deaths of Molay's chief antagonists as fully justified in the eyes of

God. I afterwards wrote five simple words in my chronicle - *'an eye for an eye.'*

After the death of the French king I travelled to the Spanish Balearic Islands where I now spend what is left of my life writing my Crònica.

Prior to the banishment of the Templar's, Philip expelled all Jews from France. It wasn't the first time this happened, nor would it be the last. Nine years later he permitted them to return to France, at the time it was the largest expulsion ever endured on European soil. I estimated that more than 100,000 individuals were forcibly uprooted to an uncertain future.

I contemplated why the French King had been called 'Philip the Fair,' especially as he confiscated every last denier from the 'Lombards,' better known as the 'Italian bankers in 1311. There appeared neither rhythm nor reason for his obscure title - it was meaningless. I considered calling this French King - Philip the Jackass. He had made enemies of the English, the Jews and the Italians, besides numerous other groups within Europe. Due to his greed and jealously the Knights Templar as an organization was no more and the Papacy was in disarray and chaos.

I was constantly in a foul mood and my writing, which normally gave me much cheer, offered me little comfort. I tried to make up for my melancholy by recalling those hectic days; I desperately missed Roger, or the man I knew as Roger De Flor.

I received many messages from Scotland telling me that the Bruce had selected my old friend as a special emissary of the Scottish Court. The Bruce might have won a great battle at Bannockburn, but the war for Scottish Independence was far from over, and needed to secure a peace with the old enemy until he was confident that peace was obtainable on the battlefield.

His explanation of the flag, the white skull and crossbones on a black background will always be embossed on my mind. It was Roger De Flor who designed our flag that others use today as a flag of fear, but Roger's conception that the flag should be flown by all men who felt nationless and outside the rule of law. As the years passed, some called the flag, Jolly Roger, in honour my friend, Roger De Flor. Whether their assumption was correct or not I cannot say. As for his death, I have little information, all I know is this.

The Bruce sent De Flor on one too many assignments from which his peace envoy failed to return to his adopted Scotland. The Bruce's friend's true identity remained a mystery was he the man I knew who planned our treasure's safe passage from France, or was he the man I knew after his supposed assassination. No one accepted responsibility for his disappearance or murder,

217

where ever he met his end the Bruce mourned for the memory and the actions of a great fighter and friend.

Ramon Muntaner died 1336 in his beloved Ibiza.

The End

Epilogue

The Chinon Document

The following news report was reported in The 'Daily Telegraph' a prominent newspaper printed in London on the 29th October, 2007.

By reporters Richard Holt and Malcolm Moore

The 'Chinon Parchment reveals that, contrary to historical belief, the Pope found that the Templars were not heretics - even though he still disbanded the order to maintain peace with their accuser, King Philip IV the Fair" of France.

Jacques de Molay, Grand Master of the Templars, was burned at the stake in 1314 along with his aides on Philip's orders, some surviving monks fled. Some were absorbed by other orders, and over the centuries, various groups have claimed to be descended from the Templars. Some of the knights who did not manage to escape were brought before Pope Clement. Their accusers claimed that the Templars initiation ceremony, which involved 'spitting on the cross', 'denying Jesus' and kissing the lower back, navel and mouth of the man proposing them, was blasphemous. However, the knights explained that the initiation mimicked the humiliation that knights could suffer if they fell into the hands of the Saracens, while the kissing ceremony was a sign of their total obedience. The Pope ultimately cleared them of heresy, but found them guilty of lesser infractions of church law.

Barbara Frale, the Vatican historian who discovered the 'Chinon Parchment' in a box of other papers, said: For 700 years we have believed that the Templars died as cursed men, and this absolves them.' She added; 'There were a lot of faults in the order - abuses, violence ... a lot of sins - but not heresy.'

The 'Chinon Parchment,' the original artefact was discovered in the Vatican's secret archives in 2001 after it had been wrongly catalogued for more than 300 years. Reproductions have been printed on synthetic parchment with a replica of the original papal wax seal. Enfolded in a soft leather case, each copy also comes with a scholarly commentary.

The Flag
Historical facts

Roger de Flor and Ramon Muntaner were indeed Knights Templar. Roger de Flor commanded the sailing units in the order and Ramon Muntaner was a Catalan mercenary and chronicler who wrote the Crònica, a chronicle of his and De Flor's life, including his adventures as a commander in the Catalan Company. Ramon died on the Spanish island of Ibiza in 1336.

The assassination of Roger de Flor occurred in 1305 at the hands of Gircon, chief of the Alans. The life of plunder, warfare and intrigues could hardly end in any other way, but with an assassination, which was carried out at the behest of the new Emperor, Michael IX Palaeologus, the co-emperor of Byzantine. However, for the benefit of this novel I needed a hero figure and De

Flor was certainly the outstanding candidate. Hence everything, please remember everything after the year 1305 mentioning Roger de Flor is sadly pure fiction.

Legend has it that the Jolly Roger obtained its appellation from the French name for a red flag turned black by De Flor, the Jolie Rouge; And so it may be, for the flag was first used by a French order of militant monks known as the 'Poor Soldiers of Christ and the Temple of Solomon - commonly known as the Knights Templar.

The Templars were pious men, giving up all their worldly possessions upon entering the Order, only carrying money on special occasions when travelling alone, reimbursing whatever money that remained upon reaching their destination. They were ferocious warriors; pitching themselves into the midst of their enemies, astride charging warhorses, against incredible odds. Contemporaries had this to say of the Templars.

The Templars were excellent soldiers. They wore white mantles with a red cross, and when they went to war a standard of two colours called balzaus was carried before them. They advanced in silence. Their first attack was the most terrible. In going, they were the first. In return, they were lost and only accepted orders from their Superiours. When they thought fit to make war and the trumpet sounded, they sang in chorus the Psalm of

David, "*Not unto us, O Lord*" kneeling on the blood and necks of the enemy, until they forced the enemy to retire altogether, or utterly broken them to pieces. Should any of them for any reason turn his back to the enemy, or come forth alive, from a defeat, or bear arms against the Christians, he was severely punished; the white mantle with the red cross, is the sign of his knighthood, is taken away with ignominy, he was then cast out from the society of the brethren, and eats his food on the floor without a napkin for the space of one year. If the dogs molest him, he couldn't dare to drive them away. But at the end of the year, if the Master and brethren thought his penance to have been sufficient, he was restored with the belt of his former knighthood. These Templars live under a strict religious code, to obey humbly, have no private property, eat sparingly, dress meanly, and dwell in tents.

In the year 711, a mighty general named Tariq-Ibn-Ziyad led an army of 300 Arabs and 10,000 Berbers across the span to invade Spain and establish am Islamic empire that ruled for 1200 years. The name *"Gibraltar"* is the Spanish derivation of the Arabic name Jabal Ṭāriq.

St. Bernard of Clairvaux wrote - '*The warriors were gentler than lambs and fiercer than lions, wedding the mildness of the monk with the valour of the knight, so that it is difficult to decide which to call them: men to adorn the Temple of Solomon with weapons instead of gems, with shields instead of crowns of gold, with saddles and bridles instead of candelabra: eager for victory - not fame; for battle not for pomp; who abhor wasteful speech, unnecessary action, unmeasured laughter, gossip and chatter, as they despise all vain things: who, in spite of their being many, live in one house according to one rule, with one soul and one heart.'*

Jacques de Vitry wrote. - *'With the lions of war and lambs at their heart; rough knights on the battlefield, pious monks in the chapel; formidable to the enemies of Christ, with gentleness itself towards his friends.'*

Ray Hudson wrote to me on July 2019 explaining, *'For me both these extractions confirm the duality symbolised in the Templar Seal.'*

Being men of principle; their rules of conduct were strict. They were willing to die for their beliefs, and so were feared on the battlefield and respected in life. Such was their reputation, that in battle, there were instances where the enemy would turn and run at the very sight of Templars entering the field of battle. Their Rule of Order stated that breaking rank was worthy of losing one's habit. They neither asked nor gave quarter; they were expected to fight until death stayed their sword arm. The retreat from an enemy would not be countenanced unless the odds were greater than three to one against them and they were forbidden to ransom themselves if captured. They fought like men possessed, either prevailing in their cause, or suffering death under the banner of Gol'gotha - the place of the skull - where Christ died.

Templars were not to succumb to the temptation of thinking that they killed in a spirit of hate and fury, nor that they seized booty in a spirit of greed. For the Templars did not hate men, but men's wrongdoing.

They were dedicated to the protection of travellers and pilgrims of all religions, though they themselves were Christians, in fact, many Templars were of Palestinian birth, spoke perfect Arabic, and were familiar with every religious sect, cult, and magical doctrine, including that of the Islamic Assassins. The Grand Master Philip of Nablus was a Syrian. They were great statesmen, politically adept economic traders, and they were allied with the great sailor-fraternity that had created a worldwide trading empire in Phoenician times. They became immensely powerful - had the largest fleet and the most successful banking system in Europe. But they could not sustain their grip on the Holy Land. Their losses were too great, and they were eventually driven off the Levant by Saladin, their Moslem adversary, in 1291. They continued to fight for their cause in the only manner they could - on the high seas.

The best known Templar pirate ship was the *'Falcon,'* the greatest that had been built at that time. She was in the harbour when the fortress at Acre fell. They rescued many ladies and damsels and great treasure together with many important people by evacuating them to Atlit.

After the orderly naval evacuation of Atlit, the Templars retreated to their Mediterranean island bases in Cyprus, Malta, Rhodes and Sicily. Until their dissolution, they, together with the Order of St. John, continued as the foremost maritime powers in the Mediterranean, and continued to wage war on all Muslim shipping.

The Templars were very powerful but in the eyes of European monarchs and the Church, the Templars raison d'tre had ceased with the loss of the Holy Lands. Jealousy and covetousness reigned. Phillip IV, who was deeply in debt to the Order, had seen their treasures stored in Paris, and designed to make it his own.

On Friday morning, October 13th 1307 - and the reason for which Friday the 13th has become known as an unlucky day - King Phillip IV together with Avignonese Pope Clement V, ruthlessly suppressed the Order throughout Europe, with false accusations, arrests, torture and executions. Though they were offered commuted sentences and comfortable lives if they would renounce their Order and plead guilty to the charges, for some mysterious reason, they preferred to remain true to their principles and received their punishment.

A large number of Templars escaped that day to an uncertain future, some found safe refuge abroad. On the eve of the arrests, the entire Templar fleet mysteriously vanished from the port of La Rochelle carrying with it its vast fortune in gold, the fate of which remains a mystery to this day.

Just as one you see a terrorist, so another sees a freedom fighter, so it was with the Templars and their fleet. Wanted by the Pope and forgotten by many of the heads of Europe, they came to be viewed as pirates; plundered the wealth of any Catholic country venturing out onto the high seas.

After being driven out of the Holy Land and mainland Europe, they remain formidable at sea. In the fourteenth century the Templars found refuge and sanctuary in Scotland, where their graves bear witness to them having once lived and dying there. King Robert the Bruce had no interest in persecuting the Order, as the sending the Papal bull ordering him to do precisely that was never sent as Scotland was already excommunicated. To the contrary, he took advantage of their fugitive status, offering them asylum in return for their help in his war for independence against King

Edward of England. It has been suggested that the Templars were used as cavalry units and assisted Robert the Bruce's infantry at the battle of Bannockburn, south of Stirling Castle. At the time the Bruce did not have a mounted force.

As Scotland evolved through the years, so did two prominent families evolve in its history - the Sinclair's and the Stuart's? Both families are able to trace their lineage back to being members of the Knights Templar, as well as to prominent figures of the New Testament. Hugh de Payen the first Grand Master of the Templars married a Sinclair.

There is sufficient evidence to suggest that the Templar fleet travelled to North America in 1398 (nearly one hundred years before Columbus) and the Sinclair's, once settled there, at least temporarily. Connections are madeamong the towered ruins along the east coast of the United States; artefacts have been discovered in the so-called Oak Island Money Pit, and the Templar Order.

The Sinclair's (or Saint-Clairs) castle near Edinburgh was situated next to Rosslyn chapel, which was constructed by order of the Sinclair family, the chapel's floor plan is supposed to bear resemblance to King Solomon's original temple. Engraved in the masonry around the chapel are maize and aloe plants, which grew only in North America.

Throughout Scotland, as well as within Rosslyn Chapel, there are carvings and tombstones dating back to the 15th, 16th, and 17th century using combinations of Templar imagery, the skull and crossbones, Templar swords, Templar crosses and Masonic symbols - principally the compasses and the square.

The royal house of Stuart became one of Freemasonry's biggest supporters during their reigns and the union between Scotland and England.

Some also suggest that the rituals used in modern Freemasonry have their origins in the ancient texts discovered by the Templar in the ruins of Solomon's Temple while excavating the building of stables. Recent archaeological digs in the area have supported this theory by finding several Templar artefacts buried beneath the temple. In the 1950's, a scroll made entirely of copper was discovered in a cave near Qumran. When translated alongside other Dead Sea Scrolls, this Copper Scroll, as it has become known, was identified as being a treasure map listing various precious metals, religious artefacts, and writings supposedly buried beneath the temple in Jerusalem.

During the 17th and 18th centuries, the skull and crossbones had become a powerful symbol with a dominate reputation identified beyond the control of any official organisation. The Templars had long since gone underground and evolved into other organisations. The symbol was usurped and came to be associated with the pirates of which we are more familiar.

They changed the flag to suit their respective needs replacing the crossbones with crossed swords, and adding hourglasses or other symbols beneath the basic skull.

Islam is an Abrahamic, monotheistic, universal religion teaching that there is only one God, and that Muhammad was a messenger of God. It is the world's second largest religion with over 1.8 billion followers or 24% of the world's population, and is most commonly known as Muslim.

Judaism, the oldest, Christianity and Islam, are the three major monotheistic religions. All originating from what we know as today as the Arab World or the Middle East. Abraham is traditionally considered to be the first Jew to have made a covenant with God. Because Judaism, Christianity, and Islam all recognise Abraham as the first prophet, thus we are all called the Abrahamic religions.

Monotheism literally means, *'the belief in only one God.'*

Roger de Flor did command a Knights Templar ship called the *'Falcon'*. There were rumours that he used that office to enrich himself, charging civilians for their rescue from any embattled city. As a result, De Flor was expelled from the Order of the Knights Templar. He went on to command a fleet of ships for Charles of Naples, who was involved in a war with Aragon over Sicily. When Charles was unable to pay for his mercenaries, Roger de Flor offered his crews' rich spoils in Syria.

It is a fact that Roger De Flor joined the Templar fleet at the age of eight. His seniority within the fleet is true.

The sinister role carried out by King Philip IV of France and Pope Clement V is also true.

The execution of nearly three thousand Muslim hostages at Acre, on the orders of Richard Plantagenet is also true.

Mount Tariq and the Pillars of Hercules existed, it is known today as the Straits of Gibraltar.

Amerigo Vespucci was born on the ninth of March, 1454 in Florence; he was an Italian explorer, financier, navigator, and cartographer. Vespucci demonstrated that Brazil and the West Indies were not Asia's eastern outskirts as initially conjectured from Columbus' voyages, but a separate, unexplored land mass colloquially known as the New World. It came to be called the Americas, a name derived from Americus, the Latin version of Vespucci's first name.

A pig in a poke - An English colloquialism meaning be careful when buying or selling without the buyer knowing its true nature or value, especially when buying without inspecting the item beforehand. In this case the piglet could turn out to be a kitten and the poke was an abbreviation for a pocket.

The Phoenicians were very skilled sailors, traders and shipbuilders, who, in their haste of management and the pursuit of efficiency, gave the world one of its greatest gifts: The modern alphabet system. The Phoenicians were members of an ancient Semitic people of North West Syria who dominated the trade of the ancient world in the first millennium BC founding colonies throughout the Mediterranean.

'The Sovereign'
A typical Templar ship

During the canonization process employed by the Roman Catholic Church, the *Promoter of the Faith*, popularly known as the Devil's advocate was a canon lawyer appointed by Church authorities to argue against the canonization of a candidate.

Plenty of proverbs and expressions warn against procrastination or ill-preparedness to which you can add this proverb. *Whet* here means "to sharpen," and the trumpet that's being blown is a military one signalling the start of a battle. Put another way, you should always be prepared: It's too late to sharpen your sword after the battle has started.

As proverbs and sayings go, you can't get much stranger than a urinating fox. Apparently, the origin of this expression refers to the fact that the fox's actions would make the ice, steam thereby fooling the fox into thinking he could produce fire. As a result, this old adage, which dates back to the 1600s, refers to someone who unrealistically expects too much of a plan or undertaking that is liable not to succeed.

What goes around comes around, or - 'as you sow, so shall you reap,' is the basic understanding of how karma, the law of cause and effect, works. The word karma literally means *'activity.'* Karma can be divided up into a few simple categories - good, bad, individual and collective. Another definition is if someone treats other people badly he or she will eventually be treated badly by someone else you should not mistreat them.

Full of wind and vinegar, the latter is usually taken to mean empty talk, full of bombast. Vinegar has always been associated with sourness and acidity in many other citations. In some cases the expression changes 'to wind and piss.'

The idiomatic phrase to stick out or to stand out, like a sore thumb is to be very obviously different from the surrounding people or things; it is especially used for someone or something that is repulsive or unwelcome.

'Apt,' quote by Alfred Adler an Austrian Psychologist (1870-1937), with reference to the fictional discussion between De Flor and Solomon on page 84 - *'It is always easier to fight for one's principles than to live up to them.'*

Feudal Usages or Feudalism was a combination of legal and military customs in medieval Europe that flourished between the 9th and 15th centuries. Broadly defined, it was a way of structuring society around relationships derived from the holding of land in exchange for service or labour.

A curia is an official body that governs a particular Church in the Catholic Church. These curia's range from the relatively simple diocesan curia, to the larger patriarchal curia's, to the Roman Curia, which is the central government of the Catholic Church.

Whether Molay's calling for revenge at the point of his agonizing death had any actual effect as a curse against his persecutors is debatable, but in an extraordinary coincidental turn of fate or bad luck, Pope Clement died just thirty-three days after Molay's execution. Seven months later King Philip himself became gravely ill and unexpectedly passed away on the 29th of November. Over the next decade, the Capetian dynasty of which King Philip was a part of staggered to its end as each of Philip's childless sons briefly became King and died. Whether or not one believes in Jacques de Molay's curse as divine retribution, however there is no doubting the calamity France faced after the Templar' downfall as the Kingdom's internecine convulsions led to the Hundred Years' War with England.

The descendants of King Philip became known as the 'Accursed Kings' reinforcing the mythology revolving around Jacques de Molay's curse.

In ancient times the *'tau'* was used as a symbol for life or resurrection, whereas the eighth letter of the Greek alphabet *'theta'* was considered the symbol of death. Tau is the last letter of the Hebrew alphabet, which was, in the old writing, shaped like a cross in the form of a 'T.' it was written in the Old Testament the tau was as a symbol of security and belonging. The tau cross was adopted by the early Christians, as its shape was reminiscent of the cross on which Jesus was crucified.

The allusion in this simile is unclear, but it seems to have originated in Britain, where rainy weather is a normal fact of life. Indeed W.L. Phelps wrote the expression 'right as rain' must have been invented by an Englishman. Its earliest recorded was in 1894, nearly six hundred years after De Flor fictionally muttered that most truthful of English sayings.

The poem as shown on page 148-149 is from the Anglo-Saxon chronicles regarding 'The Battle of Maldon' where Earl Byrhtnoth and his warriors defeated a Danish invasion led by Olaf Tryggvason.

The most famous Templar Pirate was Roger de Flor (1266-1306). He was also the most famous Templar who was a Templar Sergeant, and not a knight. Roger de Flor (also known by his original German name of Rutger von Blume) was a captain in the Templar fleet. After he was banished from the Order on charges of extorting money from passengers during the siege of Acre in 1291, Roger fled to Genoa, where he borrowed a considerable sum from Ticino Doria, purchased a new vessel and flourished in his new career as a pirate.

There's no question that the Knights Templar provoked intrigue and fascination that will probably continue until the end of time regarding any blood line. This theory is non-existent, as the Blood line was preserved by Rex Deus not the Templars.

Many academics now believe that the Turin Shroud was a forgery via the Camera Obscura by Leonardo Da Vinci. An excellent book on this is "The Divine Deception" by Dr. Keith Laidler.

Many academics now believe that the Turin Shroud is a forgery via the Camera Obscura by Leonardo

Da Vinci. An excellent book on this is "The Divine Deception" by Dr. Keith Laidler.

The dominant view within Christianity has it that God does not deceive, but there is a minority tradition within Christianity according to which God sometimes engages in intentional deception and is morally justified in doing so. This chapter draws on this minority tradition, together with sceptical theism, to raise doubts about the following thesis: God's testimony that all who believe in Jesus will have eternal life provides recipients of that testimony with a knowledge-sufficient degree of warrant for the belief that all who believe in Jesus will have eternal life. First, it is argued that there are possible situations in which divine deception is morally permissible.

YHSVH. Is displayed on the altar cloth at a Rose Croix meeting, and is the origin of Jesus being called The Son of God).

Plague epidemics ravaged Europe between the 6th and the 17th centuries. The first known outbreak in Scotland in 669 appears to have been contained; it affected only the Lothian's. Other outbreaks were recorded between 1349-50 and 1362. As various other pandemics were rife throughout Europe, I have chosen to invent an outbreak in 1312 to coincide with this, the time line of this short novel

Musselburgh was at one time the largest settlement in East Lothian, on the southern coast of the Firth of Forth. Many Scottish rivers, including the Rivers Forth and Leith flow into the Firth of Forth. It meets the North Sea with Fife on the north coast and Lothian on the south. It was known as Bodotria in Roman times. In the Norse sagas it was known as the Myrkvifiörd.

The true name of the Templars was Knights of Christ in the Temple of Solomon in Jerusalem. The name was taken from the stables granted to them by the King of Jerusalem, which were believed to have been the temple of King Solomon. The name was eventually shortened to the Knights Templar, which is definitely a lot more memorable and much easier to say.

Rosslyn Chapel was founded on a small hill what is now Roslin Cemetery above Roslin Glen as a Catholic collegiate church, with between four and six ordained canons and two boy choristers, in 1446. The chapel was founded by William Sinclair, the first Earl of Caithness and third Earl of Orkney of the Scoto-Norman Sinclair family. Rosslyn Chapel is the third Sinclair place of worship at Roslin, the first being in Roslin Castle and the second, whose crumbling buttresses can still be seen today, in what is now called the Roslin Cemetery.

On the 22nd January 1506, one hundred and ninety-nine years after the arrest of Jacques de Molay in

France, the Vatican created the Pontifical Swiss Guard. One hundred and fifty Swiss soldiers under the command of Captain Kasparvon Silenen of Canton Uri passed through the Vatican and were blessed by Pope Julius II. The famous cross associated with the Knights Templar, is incorporated into the flag of Switzerland.

It has been claimed by modern historians that Robert the Bruce was not a great military leader and could not win his own battles without help. They point again to Wallace having to lead the charge against the English to get the Bruce to this point, and that Robert had failed a reported six times and had nearly given up before the seventh time when he won. At the Battle of Bannockburn, it has been widely accepted that the Templars turned the tide of the battle in the Bruce's favour.

After the Scottish Reformation in 1560, Catholic worship in the chapel was brought to an end. The Sinclair family continued to be Catholics until the early 18th century. From that time, the chapel was closed for public worship until 1861. It was re-opened as a place of worship according to the rites of the Scottish Episcopal Church, a member church of the Anglican Communion.

The name Canada most likely comes from the Huron-Iroquois word 'Kanata,' meaning a 'village' or 'settlement.'

Please note chapter 17 is complete fiction, except for the fact that Ramon Muntaner died on the Spanish Island of Ibiza.

Roger De For

Printed in Great Britain
by Amazon

27787875R00136